James Whitcomb Riley

Pipes o'Pan at Zekesbury

James Whitcomb Riley

Pipes o'Pan at Zekesbury

ISBN/EAN: 9783743463646

Manufactured in Europe, USA, Canada, Australia, Japa

Cover: Foto ©Andreas Hilbeck / pixelio.de

Manufactured and distributed by brebook publishing software (www.brebook.com)

James Whitcomb Riley

Pipes o'Pan at Zekesbury

Pipes O' Pan at Zekesbury

Books By
James Whitcomb Riley

◆ ◆ ◆

NEGHBORLY POEMS

SKETCHES IN PROSE WITH INTERLUDING VERSES

AFTERWHILES

PIPES O' PAN AT ZEKESBURY (Prose and Verse)

RHYMES OF CHILDHOOD

THE FLYING ISLANDS OF THE NIGHT

GREEN FIELDS AND RUNNING BROOKS

ARMAZINDY

A CHILD-WORLD

HOME-FOLKS

HIS PA'S ROMANCE (Portrait by Clay)

———

GREENFIELD EDITION

Sold only in sets. Eleven volumes uniformly bound in sage-green cloth, gilt top......................................$13.50
The same in half-calf.................................. 27.00

———

OLD-FASHIONED ROSES (English Edition)

THE GOLDEN YEAR (English Edition)

POEMS HERE AT HOME

RUBÁIYÁT OF DOC SIFERS

THE BOOK OF JOYOUS CHILDREN

RILEY CHILD-RHYMES (Pictures by Vawter)

RILEY LOVE-LYRICS (Pictures by Dyer)

RILEY FARM-RHYMES (Pictures by Vawter)

RILEY SONGS O' CHEER (Pictures by Vawter)

AN OLD SWEETHEART OF MINE (Pictures by Christy)

OUT TO OLD AUNT MARY'S (Pictures by Christy)

A DEFECTIVE SANTA CLAUS (Forty Pictures by Relyea and Vawter)

PIPES O' PAN
AT ZEKESBURY

JAMES WHITCOMB RILEY

INDIANAPOLIS
THE BOBBS-MERRILL COMPANY
PUBLISHERS

PRESS OF
BRAUNWORTH & CO.
BOOKBINDERS AND PRINTERS
BROOKLYN, N. Y.

TO

MY BROTHER

JOHN A. RILEY

WITH MANY MEMORIES

OF THE OLD

HOME

CONTENTS

Pipes O' Pan at Zekesbury

THE PIPES OF PAN! Not idler now are they
Than when their cunning fashioner first blew
The pith of music from them: Yet for you
And me their notes are blown in many a way
Lost in our murmurings for that old day
That fared so well without us.—Waken to
The pipings here at hand:—The clear halloo
Of truant-voices, and the roundelay
The waters warble in the solitude
Of blooming thickets, where the robin's breast
Sends up such ecstacy o'er dale and dell,
Each tree top answers, till in all the wood
There lingers not one squirrel in his nest
Whetting his hunger on an empty shell.

AT ZEKESBURY.

THE little town, as I recall it, was of just enough dignity and dearth of the same to be an ordinary county seat in Indiana—"The Grand Old Hoosier State," as it was used to being howlingly referred to by the forensic stump orator from the old stand in the court-house yard—a political campaign being the wildest delight that Zekesbury might ever hope to call its own.

Through years the fitful happenings of the town and its vicinity went on the same—the same! Annually about one circus ventured in, and vanished, and was gone, even as a passing trumpet-blast; the usual rainy-season swelled the "Crick," the driftage choking at "the covered bridge," and backing water till the old road looked amphibious; and crowds of curious townsfolk straggled down to look upon the watery wonder, and lean awe-struck above it, and spit in it, and turn mutely home again.

The usual formula of incidents peculiar to an uneventful town and its vicinity: The countryman from "Jessup's Crossing," with the cornstalk coffin-measure, loped into town, his steaming little gray-and-red-flecked "roadster" gurgitating, as it were, with that mysterious utterance that ever has commanded and ever must evoke the wonder and bewilderment of every boy. The small-pox rumor became prevalent betimes, and the subtle aroma of the assafœtida-bag permeated the graded schools "from turret to foundation-stone;" the still recurring exposé of the poor-house management; the farm-hand, with the scythe across his shoulder, struck dead by lightning; the long-drawn quarrel between the rival editors culminating in one of them assaulting the other with a "sidestick," and the other kicking the one down stairs and thenceward *ad libitum;* the tramp, suppositiously stealing a ride, found dead on the railroad; the grand jury returning a sensational indictment against a bar-tender *non est;* the Temperance outbreak; the "Revival;" the Church Festival; and the "Free Lectures on Phrenology, and Marvels of Mesmerism," at the town hall. It was during the time of the last-mentioned sensation, and directly through this scientific investigation, that I came upon two of the town's most remarkable characters. And however meager my outline of them may prove, my material for the sketch is most accurate in every detail.

and no deviation from the cold facts of the case shall influence any line of my report.

For some years prior to this odd experience I had been connected with a daily paper at the state capitol; and latterly a prolonged session of the legislature, where I specially reported, having told threateningly upon my health, I took both the advantage of a brief vacation, and the invitation of a young bachelor Senator, to get out of the city for awhile, and bask my respiratory organs in the revivifying rural air of Zekesbury—the home of my new friend.

"It'll pay you to get out here," he said, cordially, meeting me at the little station, "and I'm glad you've come, for you'll find no end of odd characters to amuse you." And under the very pleasant sponsorship of my senatorial friend, I was placed at once on genial terms with half the citizens of the little town— from the shirt-sleeved nabob of the county office to the droll wag of the favorite loafing-place—the rules and by-laws of which resort, by the way, being rudely charcoaled on the wall above the cutter's bench, and somewhat artistically culminating in an original dialectic legend which ran thus:

F'rinstance, now whar *some* folks gits
To relyin' on their wits,

Ten to one they git too smart,
And spile it all right at the start!—
Feller wants to jest go slow
And do his *thinkin'* first, you know:—
Ef I can't think up somepin' good,
I set still and chaw my cood!

And it was at this inviting rendezvous, two
or three evenings following my arrival, that
the general crowd, acting upon the random
proposition of one of the boys, rose as a man
and wended its hilarious way to the town
hall.

"Phrenology," said the little, old, bald-
headed lecturer and mesmerist, thumbing the
egg-shaped head of a young man I remembered to have met that afternoon in some law
office; "Phrenology," repeated the professor—
"or rather the *term* phrenology—is derived
from two Greek words signifying *mind* and *dis-
course;* hence we find embodied in phrenology-
proper, the science of intellectual measure-
ment, together with the capacity of intelligent
communication of the varying mental forces
and their flexibilities, etc., &c. The study,
then, of phrenology is, to wholly simplify it—is,
I say, the general contemplation of the work-
ings of the mind as made manifest through
the certain corresponding depressions and
protuberances of the human skull, when, of
course, in a healthy state of action and devel-

opment, as we here find the conditions exemplified in the subject before us."

Here the "subject" vaguely smiled.

"You recognize that mug, don't you?" whispered my friend. "It's that coruscating young ass, you know, Hedrick—in Cummings' office—trying to study law and literature at the same time, and tampering with 'The Monster that Annually,' don't you know?—where we found the two young students scuffling round the office, and smelling of peppermint?—Hedrick, you know, and Sweeney. Sweeney, the slim chap, with the pallid face, and frog-eyes, and clammy hands! You remember I told you 'there was a pair of 'em?' Well, they're up to something here to-night. Hedrick, there on the stage in front; and Sweeney—don't you see?—with the gang on the rear seats."

"Phrenology—again," continued the lecturer, "is, we may say, a species of mental geography, as it were; which—by a study of the skull—leads also to a study of the brain within, even as geology naturally follows the initial contemplation of the earth's surface. The brain, thurfur, or intellectual retort, as we may say, natively exerts a molding influence on the skull contour; thurfur is the expert in phrenology most readily enabled to accurately locate the multitudinous intellectual forces, and

2

most exactingly estimate, as well, the sequent character of each subject submitted to his scrutiny. As, in the example before us—a young man, doubtless well known in your midst, though, I may say, an entire stranger to myself—I venture to disclose some characteristic trends and tendencies, as indicated by this phrenological depression and development of the skull-proper, as later we will show, through the mesmeric condition, the accuracy of our mental diagnosis."

Throughout the latter part of this speech my friend nudged me spasmodically, whispering something which was jostled out of intelligent utterance by some inward spasm of laughter.

"In this head," said the Professor, straddling his malleable fingers across the young man's bumpy brow—"In this head we find Ideality large — abnormally large, in fact; thurby indicating—taken in conjunction with a like development of the perceptive qualities—language following, as well, in the prominent eye—thurby indicating, I say, our subject as especially endowed with a love for the beautiful—the sublime—the elevating—the refined and delicate—the lofty and superb—in nature, and in all the sublimated attributes of the human heart and beatific soul. In fact, we find this young man possessed of such

natural gifts as would befit him for the exalted
career of the sculptor, the actor, the artist, or
the poet—any ideal calling; in fact, any calling but a practical, matter-of-fact vocation;
though in poetry he would seem to best suc-
ceed."

"Well," said my friend, seriously, "he's
feeling for the boy!" Then laughingly:
"Hedrick *has* written some rhymes for the
county papers, and Sweeney once introduced
him, at an Old Settlers' Meeting, as 'The
Best Poet in Center Township,' and never
cracked a smile! Always after each other
that way, but the best friends in the world.
Sweeney's strong suit is elocution. He has a
native ability that way by no means ordinary,
but even that gift he abuses and distorts
simply to produce grotesque, and oftentimes
ridiculous effects. For instance, nothing more
delights him than to 'lothfully' consent to
answer a request, at The Mite Society, some
evening, for 'an appropriate selection,' and
then, with an elaborate introduction of the
same, and an exalted tribute to the refined
genius of the author, proceed with a most
gruesome rendition of 'Alonzo The Brave and
The Fair Imogene,' in a way to coagulate the
blood and curl the hair of his fair listeners
with abject terror. Pale as a corpse, you

know, and with that cadaverous face, lit with
those malignant-looking eyes, his slender figure, and his long, thin legs and arms and
hands, and his whole diabolical talent and
adroitness brought into play—why, I want to
say to you, it 's enough to scare 'em to death!
Never a smile from him, though, till he and
Hedrick are safe out into the night again—
then, of course, they hug each other and howl
over it like Modocs! But pardon; I 'm inter-
rupting the lecture.   Listen."

"A lack of continuity, however," continued
the Professor, "and an undue love of appro-
bation, would, measurably, at least, tend to
retard the young man's progress toward the
consummation of any loftier ambition, I fear;
yet as we have intimated, if the subject were
appropriately educated to the need's demand,
he could doubtless produce a high order of
both prose and poetry—especially the latter—
though he could very illy bear being laughed
at for his pains."

" He 's dead wrong there," said my friend;
" Hedrick enjoys being laughed at; he 's used
to it—gets fat on it!"

" Is fond of his friends," continued the Professor " and the heartier they are the better:
might even be convivially inclined—if so
tempted—but prudent—in a degree," loiter-

ingly concluded the speaker, as though unable to find the exact bump with which to bolster up the last named attribute.

The subject blushed vividly—my friend's right eyelid dropped, and there was a noticeable, though elusive sensation throughout the audience.

"*But!*" said the Professor, explosively, "selecting a directly opposite subject, in conjunction with the study of the one before us [turning to the group at the rear of the stage and beckoning], we may find a newer interest in the practical comparison of these subjects side by side." And the Professor pushed a very pale young man into position.

"Sweeney!" whispered my friend, delightedly; "now look out!"

"In *this* subject," said the Professor, "we find the practical business head. Square—though small—a trifle light at the base, in fact; but well balanced at the important points at least; thoughtful eyes—wide-awake—crafty—quick—restless—a policy eye, though not denoting language—unless, perhaps, mere business forms and direct statements."

"Fooled again!" whispered my friend; "and I'm afraid the old man will fail to nest out the fact also that Sweeney is the cold-bloodedest guyer on the face of the earth, and with more diabolical resources than a prosecuting attorney ; the Professor ought to know this, too, by this time—for these same two chaps have been visiting the old man in his room at the hotel ;—that's what I was trying to tell you awhile ago. The old sharp thinks he's ' playing ' the boys, is my idea ; but it's the other way, or I lose my guess."

" Now, under the mesmeric influence—if the two subjects will consent to its administration," said the Professor, after some further tedious preamble, " we may at once determine the fact of my assertions, as will be proved by their action while in this peculiar state." Here some apparent remonstrance was met with from both subjects, though amicably overcome by the Professor first manipulating the stolid brow and pallid front of the imperturbable Sweeney—after which the same mysterious ordeal was lothfully submitted to by Hedrick— though a noticeably longer time was consumed in securing his final loss of self-control. At last, however, this curious phenomenon was presented, and there before us stood the two swaying figures, the heads dropped back, the lifted hands, with thumb and finger-tips pressed lightly together, the eyelids languid and half closed, and the features, in appearance, wan and humid.

"Now, sir!" said the Professor, leading the limp Sweeney forward, and addressing him in a quick, sharp tone of voice.—"Now, sir, you are a great contractor—own large factories, and with untold business interests. Just look out there! [pointing out across the expectant audience] look there, and see the countless minions toiling servilely at your dread mandates. And yet—ha! ha! See! see!—-They recognize the avaricious greed that would thus grind them in the very dust; they see, alas! they see themselves half-clothed—half-fed, that you may glut your coffers. Half-starved, they listen to the wail of wife and babe, and, with eyes upraised in prayer, they see *you* rolling by in gilded coach, and swathed in silk attire. But—ha! again! Look—look! they are rising in revolt against you! Speak to them before too late! Appeal to them—quell them with the promise of the just advance of wages they demand!"

The limp figure of Sweeney took on something of a stately and majestic air. With a graceful and commanding gesture of the hand, he advanced a step or two; then, after a pause of some seconds duration, in which the lifted face grew paler, as it seemed, and the eyes a denser black, he said:

> "But yesterday
> I looked away
> O'er happy lands, where sunshine lay
> In golden blots,
> Inlaid with spots
> Of shade and wild forget-me-nots."

The voice was low, but clear, and ever musical. The Professor started at the strange utterance, looked extremely confused, and, as the boisterous crowd cried "Hear, hear!" he motioned the subject to continue, with some gasping comment interjected, which, if audible, would have run thus: "My God! It's an inspirational poem!"

> "My head was fair
> With flaxen hair——"

resumed the subject.

"Yoop-ee!" yelled an irreverent auditor.

"Silence! silence!" commanded the excited Professor in a hoarse whisper; then, turning enthusiastically to the subject—"Go on, young man! Go on!—'*Thy head was fair with flaxen hair*——'"

> "My head was fair
> With flaxen hair,
> And fragrant breezes, faint and rare,
> And warm with drouth
> From out the south,
> Blew all my curls across my mouth."

The speaker's voice, exquisitely modulated, yet resonant as the twang of a harp, now seemed of itself to draw and hold each listener; while a certain extravagance of gesticulation—a fantastic movement of both form and feature—seemed very near akin to fascination.   And so flowed on the curious utterance:

> "And, cool and sweet,
>   My naked feet
>   Found dewy pathways through the wheat;
>   And out again
>   Where, down the lane,
>   The dust was dimpled with the rain."

In the pause following there was a breathlessness almost painful.   The poem went on:

> "But yesterday
>   I heard the lay
>   Of summer birds, when I, as they
>   With breast and wing,
>   All quivering
>   With life and love, could only sing.
>
> "My head was leant,
>   Where, with it, blent
>   A maiden's, o'er her instrument;
>   While all the night,
>   From vale to height,
>   Was filled with echoes of delight.
>
> "And all our dreams
>   Were lit with gleams

> Of that lost land of reedy streams,
> Along whose brim
> Forever swim
> Pan's lilies, laughing up at him."

And still the inspired singer held rapt sway.

"It is wonderful!" I whispered, under breath.

"Of course it is!" answered my friend. "But listen; there is more:"

> "But yesterday! . . . .
> O blooms of May,
> And summer roses—Where-away?
> O stars above;
> And lips of love,
> And all the honeyed sweets thereof!

> "O lad and lass,
> And orchard-pass,
> And briared lane, and daisied grass!
> O gleam and gloom,
> And woodland bloom,
> And breezy breaths of all perfume!—

> "No more for me
> Or mine shall be
> Thy raptures —save in memory,—
> No more—no more—
> Till through the Door
> Of Glory gleam the days of yore."

This was the evident conclusion of the re-markable utterance, and the Professor was impetuously fluttering his hands about the

subject's upward-staring eyes, stroking his
temples, and snapping his fingers in his face.

"Well," said Sweeney, as he stood suddenly awakened, and grinning in an idiotic
way, "how did the old thing work?" And it
was in the consequent hilarity and loud and
long applause, perhaps, that the Professor was
relieved from the explanation of this rather
astounding phenomenon of the idealistic work-
ings of a purely practical brain—or, as my
impious friend scoffed the incongruity later,
in a particularly withering allusion, as the
"blank-blanked fallacy, don't you know, of
staying the hunger of a howling mob by feed-
ing 'em on Spring poetry!"

The tumult of the audience did not cease
even with the retirement of Sweeney, and
cries of "Hedrick! Hedrick!" only subsided
with the Professor's high-keyed announcement that the subject was even then endeav-
oring to make himself heard, but could not
until utter quiet was restored, adding the further appeal that the young man had already
been a long time under the mesmeric spell, and
ought not be so detained for an unnecessary
period. "See," he concluded, with an as-
suring wave of the hand toward the subject,
"see; he is about to address you. Now,
quiet!—utter quiet, if you please!"

"Great heavens!" exclaimed my friend, stiflingly; "Just look at the boy! Get onto that position for a poet! Even Sweeney has fled from the sight of him!"

And truly, too, it was a grotesque pose the young man had assumed; not wholly ridiculous either, since the dwarfed position he had settled into seemed more a genuine physical condition than an affected one. The head, back-tilted, and sunk between the shoulders, looked abnormally large, while the features of the face appeared peculiarly child-like— especially the eyes—wakeful and wide apart, and very bright, yet very mild and very artless; and the drawn and cramped outline of the legs and feet, and of the arms and hands, even to the shrunken, slender-looking fingers, all combined to most strikingly convey to the pained senses the fragile frame and pixey figure of some pitiably afflicted child, unconscious altogether of the pathos of its own deformity.

"Now, mark the kuss, Horatio!" gasped my friend.

At first the speaker's voice came very low, and somewhat piping, too, and broken—an eerie sort of voice it was, of brittle and erratic *timbre* and undulant inflection. Yet it was beautiful. It had the ring of childhood in it,

though the ring was not pure golden, and at
times fell echoless. The *spirit* of its utterance was always clear and pure and crisp
and cheery as the twitter of a bird, and yet
forever ran an undercadence through it like a
low-pleading prayer. Half garrulously, and
like a shallow brook might brawl across a
shelvy bottom, the rhythmic little changeling
thus began :

"I 'm thist a little crippled boy, an' never goin' to grow
  An' git a great big man at all!—'cause Aunty told me so.
  When I was thist a baby onc't I falled out of the bed
  An' got 'The Curv'ture of the Spine'—'at 's what the
    Doctor said.
  I never had no Mother nen—fer my Pa runned away
  An' dass n't come back here no more—'cause he was
    drunk one day
  An' stobbed a man In thish-ere town, an' could n't pay
    his fine!
  An' nen my Ma she died—an' I got 'Curv'ture of the
    Spine!'"

A few titterings from the younger people
in the audience marked the opening stanza,
while a certain restlessness, and a changing
to more attentive positions seemed the general
tendency. The old Professor, in the mean-
time, had sunk into one of the empty chairs.
The speaker went on with more gaiety :

"I 'm nine years old! An' you can 't guess how much I
  weigh, I bet!—

Last birthday I weighed thirty-three!—An' I weigh
  thirty yet!
I 'm awful little fer my size—I 'm purt' nigh littler 'an
Some babies is!—an' neighbors all calls me 'The Little
  Man!'
An' Doc one time he laughed an' said: 'I 'spect, first
  thing you know,
You 'll have a little spike-tail coat an' travel with a
  show!'
An' nen I laughed—till I looked round an' Aunty was
  a-cryin'—
Sometimes she acts like that, 'cause I got 'Curv'ture of
  the Spine!'"

Just in front of me a great broad-shouldered
countryman, with a rainy smell in his cum-
brous overcoat, cleared his throat vehemently,
looked startled at the sound, and again settled forward, his weedy chin resting on the
knuckles of his hands as they tightly clutched
the seat before him. And it was like being
taken into a childish confidence as the quaint
speech continued:

"I set—while Aunty 's washin'—on my little long-leg
  stool,
  An' watch the little boys an' girls 'a-skippin' by to
    school;
  An' I peck on the winder, an' holler out an' say:
'Who wants to fight The Little Man 'at dares you all
    to-day?'
  An' nen the boys climbs on the fence, an' little girls
    peeks through,
  An' they all says: 'Cause you 're so big, you think
    we 're 'feared o' you!'

An' nen they yell, an' shake their fist at me, like I shake
    mine—
They 're thist in fun, you know, 'cause I got 'Curv'ture
    of the Spine!'"

" Well," whispered my friend, with rather
odd irrelevance, I thought, " of course you
see through the scheme of the fellows by this
time, do n't you?"

" I see nothing," said I, most earnestly,
" but a poor little wisp of a child that makes
me love him so I dare not think of his dying
soon, as he surely must! There; listen!"
And the plaintive gaiety of the homely poem
ran on:

" At evening, when the ironin's done, an' Aunty's fixed
    the fire,
  An' filled an' lit the lamp, an' trimmed the wick an'
    turned it higher,
  An' fetched the wood all in fer night, an' locked the
    kitchen door,
  An' stuffed the ole crack where the wind blows in up
    through the floor—
She sets the kittle on the coals, an' biles an' makes the
    tea,
  An' fries the liver an' the mush, an' cooks a egg fer me;
  An' sometimes—when I cough so hard—her elderberry
    wine
  Don't go so bad fer little boys with 'Curv'ture of the
    Spine!'"

" Look!" whispered my friend, touching
me with his elbow. " Look at the Professor!"

"Look at everybody!" said I. And the artless little voice went on again half quaveringly:

"But Aunty's all so childish-like on my account, you see,
　I'm 'most afeared she'll be took down—an' 'at's what
　　bothers *me!*—
　'Cause ef my good ole Aunty ever would git sick an' die,
　I don't know what she'd do in Heaven—till *I* come, by
　　an' by:—
　Fer she's so ust to all my ways, an' ever'thing, you
　　know,
　An' no one there like me, to nurse, an' worry over so!—
　'Cause all the little childerns there's so straight an' strong
　　an' fine,
　They's nary angel 'bout the place with 'Curv'ture of
　　the Spine!'"

The old Professor's face was in his handkerchief; so was my friend's in his; and so was mine in mine, as even now my pen drops and I reach for it again.

I half regret joining the mad party that had gathered an hour later in the old law-office where these two graceless characters held almost nightly revel, the instigators and conniving hosts of a reputed banquet whose *menu's* range confined itself to herrings, or "blind robins," dried beef, and cheese, with crackers, gingerbread, and sometimes pie; the whole washed down with anything but

"——Wines that heaven knows when
Had sucked the fire of some forgotten sun,
And kept it through a hundred years of gloom
Still glowing in a heart of ruby."

But the affair was memorable. The old Professor was himself lured into it, and loudest in his praise of Hedrick's realistic art; and I yet recall him at the orgie's height, excitedly repulsing the continued slurs and insinuations of the clammy-handed Sweeney, who, still contending against the old man's fulsome praise of his more fortunate rival, at last openly declared that Hedrick was *not* a poet, *not* a genius, and in no way worthy to be classed in the same breath with *himself*—" the gifted but unfortunate *Sweeney*, sir—the unacknowledged author, sir—'y gad, sir!—of the two poems that held you spell-bound to-night!"

3

Down Around the River Poems

DOWN AROUND THE RIVER.

NOON-TIME and June-time, down around the
river!
Have to furse with 'Lizey Ann—but lawzy! I fergive her!
Drives me off the place, and says 'at all 'at she 's a-wishin',
Land o' gracious! time 'll come I 'll git enough o' fishin'!
Little Dave, a-choppin' wood, never 'pears to notice;
Don't know where she 's hid his hat, er keerin' where his
        coat is,—
Specalatin', more 'n like, he haint a-goin' to mind me,
And guessin' where, say twelve o'clock, a feller 'd likely
        find me.

Noon-time and June-time, down around the river!
Clean out o' sight o' home, and skulkin' under kivver
Of the sycamores, jack-oaks, and swamp-ash and ellum—
Idies all so jumbled up, you kin hardly tell 'em!—
Tired, you know, but *lovin'* it, and smilin' jest to think 'at
Any sweeter tiredness you 'd fairly want to *drink* it.
Tired o' fishin'—tired o' fun—line out slack and slacker—
All you want in all the world 's a little more tobacker!

Hungry, but *a-hidin'* it, er jes' a-not a-keerin':—
Kingfisher gittin' up and skootin' out o' hearin';
Snipes on the t'other side, where the County Ditch is,
Wadin' up and down the aidge like they 'd rolled their
        britches!
Old turkle on the root kindo-sorto drappin'
Intoo th' worter like he do n't know how it happen!
Worter, shade and all so mixed, do n't know which you 'd
        orter
Say, th' *worter* in the shadder—*shadder* in the *worter!*

(37)

Somebody hollerin'—'way around the bend in
Upper Fork—where yer eye kin jes' ketch the endin'
Of the shiney wedge o' wake some muss-rat's a-makin'
With that pesky nose o' his!   Then a sniff o' bacon,
Corn-bread and 'dock-greens—and little Dave a-shinnin'
'Crost the rocks and mussel-shells, a-limpin' and a-grinnin',
With yer dinner fer ye, and a blessin' from the giver.
Noon-time and June-time down around the river!

DEAR LORD, to Thee my knee is bent.—
    Give me content —
Full-pleasured with what comes to me,
    What e'er it be:
An humble roof - a frugal board,
    And simple hoard;
The wintry fagot piled beside
    The chimney wide,
While the enwreathing flames up-sprout
    And twine about
The brazen dogs that guard my hearth
    And household worth:
Tinge with the ember's ruddy glow
    The rafters low;
And let the sparks snap with delight,
    As fingers might
That mark deft measures of some tune
    The children croon:
Then, with good friends, the rarest few
    Thou holdest true,
Ranged round about the blaze, to share
    My comfort there,—
Give me to claim the service meet
    That makes each seat
A place of honor, and each guest
    Loved as the rest.

ROMANCIN'.

I' B'EN a-kindo musin', as the feller says, and I 'm
   About o' the conclusion that they ain't no better time
When you come to cipher on it, than the times we used to
    know
When we swore our first "dog-gone-it" sorto solem'-like
    and low!

You git my idy, do you? – *Little* tads, you understand—
Jes' a wishin' thue and thue you that you on'y was a *man*.—
Yit here I am, this minute, even forty, to a day,
And fergittin' all that 's in it, wishin' jes' the other way!

I hain't no hand to lectur' on the times, er dimonstrate
Whur the trouble is, er hector and domineer with Fate,—
But when I git so flurried, and so pestered-like and blue,
And so rail owdacious worried, let me tell you what I do!—

I jes' gee-haw the hosses, and unhook the swingle-tree,
Whur the hazel-bushes tosses down their shadders over
    me,
And I draw my plug o' navy, and I climb the fence, and set
Jes' a-thinkin' here, 'y gravy! till my eyes is wringin'-wet!

Tho' I still kin see the trouble o' the *present*, I kin see—
Kindo like my sight was double—all the things that *used
    to be;*
And the flutter o' the robin, and the teeter o' the wren
Sets the willer branches bobbin "howdy-do" thum Now
    to Then!
The deadnin' and the thicket 's jes' a bilin' full of June,
Thum the rattle o' the cricket, to the yallar-hammer's tune;

And the catbird in the bottom, and the sap-suck on the
    snag,
Seems ef they cain't—od-rot 'em!—jes' do nothin' else but
    brag!

They's music in the twitter of the bluebird and the jay,
And that sassy little critter jes' a-peckin' all the day;
They's music in the "flicker," and they's music in the
    thrush,
And they's music in the snicker o' the chipmunk in the
    brush!

They's music *all around* me!—And I go back, in a dream—
Sweeter yit than ever found me fast asleep—and in the
    stream
That used to split the medder whur the dandylions growed,
I stand knee-deep, and redder than the sunset down the
    road.

Then's when I' b'en a-fishin'!—and they's other fellers,
    too,
With their hickry poles a-swishin' out behind 'em; and a
    few
Little "shiners" on our stringers, with their tails tiptoein'
    bloom,
As we dance 'em in our fingers all the happy journey home.

I kin see us, true to Natur', thum the time we started out
With a biscuit and a 'tater in our little "roundabout!"
I kin see our lines a-tanglin', and our elbows in a jam,
And our naked legs a-danglin' thum the apern of the dam.

I kin see the honeysuckle climbin' up around the mill;
And kin hear the worter chuckle, and the wheel a-growlin'
    still;
And thum the bank below it I kin steal the old canoe,
And jes' git in and row it like the miller used to do.

W'y, I git my fancy focussed on the past so mortal plain
I kin even smell the locus'-blossoms bloomin' in the lane;
And I hear the cow-bells clinkin' sweeter tunes 'n "money
    musk "
Fer the lightnin'-bugs a-blinkin' and a-dancin' in the dusk.

And so I keep   as the feller says, till I'm
Firm-fixed in the conclusion that they hain't no better
    time,
When you come to cipher on it, than the *old* times,—and,
    I swear,
I kin wake and say "dog-gone-it!" jes' as soft as any
    prayer!

HAS SHE FORGOTTEN.

I.

HAS SHE forgotten? On this very May
We were to meet here, with the birds and bees,
As on that Sabbath, underneath the trees
We strayed among the tombs, and stripped away
The vines from these old granites, cold and gray—
And yet, indeed, not grim enough were they
To stay our kisses, smiles and ecstacies,
Or closer voice-lost vows and rhapsodies.
Has she forgotten—that the May has won
Its promise?—that the bird-songs from the tree
Are sprayed above the grasses as the sun
Might jar the dazzling dew down showeringly?
Has she forgotten life—love—everyone—
Has she forgotten me—forgotten me?

II.

Low, low down in the violets I press
My lips and whisper to her. Does she hear,
And yet hold silence, though I call her dear,
Just as of old, save for the tearfulness
Of the clenched eyes, and the soul's vast distress?
Has she forgotten thus the old caress
That made our breath a quickened atmosphere
That failed nigh unto swooning with the sheer
Delight? Mine arms clutch now this earthen heap
Sodden with tears that flow on ceaselessly
As autumn rains the long, long, long nights weep
In memory of days that used to be,—
Has she forgotten these? And, in her sleep,
Has she forgotten me—forgotten me?

(43)

III.

To-night, against my pillow, with shut eyes,
I mean to weld our faces—through the dense
Incalculable darkness make pretense
That she has risen from her reveries
To mate her dreams with mine in marriages
Of mellow palms, smooth faces, and tense ease
Of every longing nerve of indolence,—
Lift from the grave her quiet lips, and stun
My senses with her kisses—drawl the glee
Of her glad mouth, full blithe and tenderly,
Across mine own, forgetful if is done
The old love's awful dawn-time when said we,
"To-day is ours!" . . . . Ah, Heaven! can it be
She has forgotten me—forgotten me!

A' OLD PLAYED-OUT SONG.

IT 'S THE curiousest thing in creation,
 Whenever I hear that old song,
"Do They Miss Me at Home?" I 'm so bothered,
 My life seems as short as it 's long!—
Fer ever'thing 'pears like adzackly
 It 'peared, in the years past and gone,—
When I started out sparkin', at twenty,
 And had my first neckercher on!

Though I 'm wrinkelder, older and grayer
 Right now than my parents was then,
You strike up that song, "Do They Miss Me?"
 And I 'm jest a youngster again!—
I 'm a-standin' back there in the furries
 A-wishin' fer evening to come,
And a-whisperin' over and over
 Them words, "Do They Miss Me at Home?"

You see, Marthy Ellen she sung it
 The first time I heerd it; and so,
As she was my very first sweetheart,
 It reminds of her, do n't you know,—
How her face ust to look, in the twilight,
 As I tuck her to spellin'; and she
Kep' a-hummin' that song 'tel I ast her,
 Pine-blank, ef she ever missed me!

I can shet my eyes now, as you sing it,
 And hear her low answerin' words,
And then the glad chirp of the crickets
 As clear as the twitter of birds;

(45)

And the dust in the road is like velvet,
   And the ragweed, and fennel, and grass
Is as sweet as the scent of the lilies
   Of Eden of old, as we pass.

"Do They Miss Me at Home?" Sing it lower—
   And softer—and sweet as the breeze
That powdered our path with the snowy
   White bloom of the old locus'-trees!
Let the whippoorwills he'p you to sing it,
   And the echoes 'way over the hill,
'Tel the moon boolges out, in a chorus
   Of stars, and our voices is still.

But, oh! "They's a chord in the music
   That's missed when *her* voice is away!"
Though I listen from midnight 'tel morning,
   And dawn, 'tel the dusk of the day;
And I grope through the dark, lookin' up'ards
   And on through the heavenly dome,
With my longin' soul singin' and sobbin'
   The words, "Do They Miss Me at Home?"

THE LOST PATH.

ALONE they walked—their fingers knit together
  And swaying listlessly as might a swing
Wherein Dan Cupid dangled in the weather
  Of some sun-flooded afternoon of Spring.

Within the clover-fields the tickled cricket
  Laughed lightly as they loitered down the lane,
And from the covert of the hazel-thicket
  The squirrel peeped and laughed at them again.

The bumble-bee that tipped the lily-vases
  Along the road-side in the shadows dim,
Went following the blossoms of their faces
  As though their sweets must needs be shared with him.

Between the pasture bars the wondering cattle
  Stared wistfully, and from their mellow bells
Shook out a welcoming whose dreamy rattle
  Fell swooningly away in faint farewells.

And though at last the gloom of night fell o'er them,
  And folded all the landscape from their eyes,
They only know the dusky path before them
  Was leading safely on to Paradise.

THE LITTLE TINY KICKSHAW

"—And any little tiny kickshaws."—Shakespeare.

O THE LITTLE tiny kickshaw that Mither sent
        tae me,
'Tis sweeter than the sugar-plum that reepens on the tree,
Wi' denty flavorin's o' spice an' musky rosemarie,
The little tiny kickshaw that Mither sent tae me.

'Tis luscious wi' the stalen tang o' fruits frae ower the sea,
An' e'en its fragrance gars we laugh wi' langin' lip an' ee,
Till a' its frazen sheen o' white maun melten hinnie be—
Sae weel I luve the kickshaw that Mither sent tae me.

O I luve the tiny kickshaw, an' I smack my lips wi' glee,
Aye mickle do I luve the taste o' sic a luxourie,
But maist I luve the luvein' han's that could the giftie gie
O' the little tiny kickshaw that Mither sent tae me.

HIS MOTHER.

DEAD! my wayward boy—*my own*—
Not *the Law's!* but *mine*—the good
God's free gift to me alone,
Sanctified by motherhood.

"Bad," you say: Well, who is not?
"Brutal"—"with a heart of stone"—
And "red-handed."—Ah! the hot
Blood upon your own!

I come not, with downward eyes,
To plead for him shamedly,—
God did not apologize
When He gave the boy to me.

Simply, I make ready now
For *His* verdict.—*You* prepare—
You have killed us both—and how
Will you face us There!

KISSING THE ROD.

O HEART of mine, we should n't
    Worry so!
What we 've missed of calm we could n.*
    Have, you know!
What we 've met of stormy pain,
And of sorrow's driving rain,
We can better meet again,
    If it blow!

We have erred in that dark hour
    We have known,
When our tears fell with the shower,
    All alone!—
Were not shine and shadow blent
As the gracious Master meant?—
Let us temper our content
    With His own.

For, we know, not every morrow
    Can be sad;
So, forgetting all the sorrow
    We have had,
Let us fold away our fears,
And put by our foolish tears,
And through all the coming years
    Just be glad.

HOW IT HAPPENED.

I GOT to thinkin' of her—both her parents dead and
   gone—
And all her sisters married off, and none but her and John
A-livin' all alone there in that lonesome sort o' way,
And him a blame old bachelor, confirmder ev'ry day!
I'd knowed 'em all from childern, and their daddy from
   the time
He settled in the neighborhood, and had n't ary a dime
Er dollar, when he married, fer to start housekeepin' on!—
So I got to thinkin' of her—both her parents dead and
   gone!

I got to thinkin' of her; and a-wundern what she done
That all her sisters kep' a gittin' married, one by one,
And her without no chances—and the best girl of the
   pack—
An old maid, with her hands, you might say, tied behind
   her back!
And Mother, too, afore she died, she ust to jes' take on,
When none of 'em was left, you know, but Evaline and
   John,
And jes' declare to goodness 'at the young men must be
   bline
To not see what a wife they 'd git if they got Evaline!

I got to thinkin' of her; in my great affliction she
Was sich a comfert to us, and so kind and neighberly,—
She 'd come, and leave her housework, fer to he'p out
   little Jane,
And talk of *her own* mother 'at she 'd never see again—
Maybe sometimes cry together—though, fer the most part
   she

(51)

Would have the child so riconciled and happy-like 'at we
Felt lonesomer 'n ever when she 'd put her bonnet on
And say she 'd railly haf to be a-gittin' back to John!

I got to thinkin' of her, as I say,—and more and more
I 'd think of her dependence, and the burdens 'at she bore,—
Her parents both a-bein' dead, and all her sisters gone
And married off, and her a-livin' there alone with John—
You might say jes' a-toilin' and a-slavin' out her life
Fer a man 'at hadn't pride enough to git hisse'f a wife—
'Less some one married *Evaline*, and packed her off some
    day!—
So I got to thinkin' of her—and it happened thataway.

BABYHOOD.

HEIGH-HO! Babyhood! Tell me where you linger:
  Let's toddle home again, for we have gone astray;
Take this eager hand of mine and lead me by the finger
  Back to the Lotus lands of the far-away.

Turn back the leaves of life; do n't read the story,—
  Let's find the *pictures*, and fancy all the rest:—
We can fill the written pages with a brighter glory
  Than Old Time, the story-teller, at his very best!

Turn to the brook, where the honeysuckle, tipping
  O'er its vase of perfume spills it on the breeze,
And the bee and humming-bird in ecstacy are sipping
  From the fairy flagons of the blooming locust trees.

Turn to the lane, where we used to "teeter-totter,"
  Printing little foot-palms in the mellow mold,
Laughing at the lazy cattle wading in the water
  Where the ripples dimple round the buttercups of gold:

Where the dusky turtle lies basking on the gravel
  Of the sunny sandbar in the middle-tide,
And the ghostly dragonfly pauses in his travel
  To rest like a blossom where the water-lily died.

Heigh-ho! Babyhood! Tell me where you linger:
  Let's toddle home again, for we have gone astray;
Take this eager hand of mine and lead me by the finger
  Back to the Lotus lands of the far-away.

THE DAYS GONE BY.

O THE DAYS gone by! O the days gone by!
The apples in the orchard, and the pathway through
the rye;
The chirrup of the robin, and the whistle of the quail
As he piped across the meadows sweet as any nightingale;
When the bloom was on the clover, and the blue was in
the sky,
And my happy heart brimmed over in the days gone by.

In the days gone by, when my naked feet were tripped
By the honey-suckle's tangles where the water-lilies
dipped,
And the ripples of the river lipped the moss along the brink
Where the placid-eyed and lazy-footed cattle came to
drink,
And the tilting snipe stood fearless of the truant's way-
ward cry
And the splashing of the swimmer, in the days gone by.

O the days gone by! O the days gone by!
The music of the laughing lip, the luster of the eye;
The childish faith in fairies, and Aladdin's magic ring—
The simple, soul-reposing, glad belief in everything,—
When life was like a story, holding neither sob nor sigh,
In the golden olden glory of the days gone by.

Mrs. Miller

MRS. MILLER.

JOHN B. McKINNEY, Attorney and Counselor at Law, as his sign read, was, for many reasons, a fortunate man. For many other reasons he was not. He was chiefly fortunate in being, as certain opponents often strove to witheringly designate him, "the son of his father," since that sound old gentleman was the wealthiest farmer in that section, with but one son and heir to, in time, supplant him in the role of " county god," and haply perpetuate the prouder title of " the biggest tax-payer on the assessment list." And this fact, too, fortunate as it would seem, was doubtless the indirect occasion of a liberal percentage of all John's misfortunes. From his earliest school-days in the little town, up to his tardy graduation from a distant college, the influence of his father's wealth invited his procrastination, humored its results, encouraged the laxity of his ambition, " and even now," as John used, in bitter irony, to put it, "it is aiding and abetting me in the ostensible practice of my chosen profession, a listless, aimless undetermined man of forty, and a con-

firmed bachelor at that!" At the utterance
of this self-depreciating statement, John generally jerked his legs down from the top of his
desk; and, rising and kicking his chair back
to the wall, he would stump around his littered
office till the manilla carpet steamed with dust.
Then he would wildly break away, seeking
refuge either in the open street, or in his room
at the old-time tavern, The Eagle House,
"where," he would say, "I have lodged and
boarded, I do solemnly asseverate, for a long,
unbroken, middle-aged eternity of ten years,
and can yet assert, in the words of the more
fortunately-dying Webster, that 'I still live!'"

Extravagantly satirical as he was at times,
John had always an indefinable drollery about
him that made him agreeable company to his
friends, at least; and such an admiring friend
he had constantly at hand in the person of
Bert Haines. Both were Bohemians in natural tendency, and, though John was far in
Bert's advance in point of age, he found the
young man "just the kind of a fellow to have
around;" while Bert, in turn, held his senior
in profound esteem—looked up to him, in fact,
and in even his eccentricities strove to pattern
after him. And so it was, when summer days
were dull and tedious, these two could muse and
doze the hours away together; and when the

nights were long, and dark, and deep, and
beautiful, they could drift out in the noon-
light of the stars, and with "the soft com-
plaining flute" and "warbling lute," "lay
the pipes," as John would say, for their en-
during popularity with the girls! And it was
immediately subsequent to one of these ro-
mantic excursions, when the belated pair, at
two o'clock in the morning, had skulked up
a side stairway of the old hotel, and gained
John's room, with nothing more serious hap-
pening than Bert falling over a trunk and
smashing his guitar,—just after such a night
of romance and adventure it was that, in the
seclusion of John's room, Bert had something
of especial import to communicate.

"Mack," he said, as that worthy anathe-
matized a spiteful match, and then sucked his
finger.

"Blast the all-fired old torch!" said John,
wrestling with the lamp-flue, and turning on
a welcome flame at last. "Well, you said
'Mack!' Why do n't you go on? And do n't
bawl at the top of your lungs, either. You 've
already succeeded in waking every boarder
in the house with that guitar, and you want
to make amends now by letting them go to
sleep again!"

"But my dear fellow," said Bert, with

forced calmness, "you're the fellow that's making all the noise—and—"

"Why, you howling dervish!" interrupted John, with a feigned air of pleased surprise and admiration. "But let's drop controversy. Throw the fragments of your guitar in the wood-box there, and proceed with the opening proposition."

"What I was going to say was this," said Bert, with a half-desperate enunciation; "I'm getting tired of this way of living—clean, dead-tired, and fagged out, and sick of the whole artificial business!"

"Oh, yes!" exclaimed John, with a towering disdain, "you need n't go any further! I know just what malady is throttling you. It's reform—reform! You're going to 'turn over a new leaf,' and all that, and sign the pledge, and quit cigars, and go to work, and pay your debts, and gravitate back into Sunday-School, where you can make love to the preacher's daughter under the guise of religion, and desecrate the sanctity of the innermost pale of the church by confessions at Class of your 'thorough conversion!' Oh, you're going to——"

"No, but I'm going to do nothing of the sort," interrupted Bert, resentfully. "What I mean—if you 'll let me finish—is, I 'm getting too old to be eternally undignifying myself with this 'singing of midnight strains under Bonnybell's window panes,' and too old to be keeping myself in constant humiliation and expense by the borrowing and stringing up of old guitars, together with the breakage of the same, and the general wear-and-tear on a constitution that is slowly being sapped to its foundations by exposure in the night-air and the dew." "And while you receive no further compensation in return," said John, " than, perhaps, the coy turning up of a lamp at an upper casement where the jasmine climbs ; or an exasperating patter of invisible palms ; or a huge dank wedge of fruit-cake shoved at you by the old man, through a crack in the door."

" Yes, and I 'm going to have my just reward, is what I mean," said Bert, " and exchange the lover's life for the benedict's. Going to hunt out a good, sensible girl and marry her." And as the young man concluded this desperate avowal he jerked the bow of his cravat into a hard knot, kicked his hat under the bed, and threw himself on the sofa like an old suit.

John stared at him with absolute compas-

sion. "Poor devil," he said, half musingly,
"I know just how he feels—

> 'Ring in the wind his wedding chimes,
>   Smile, villagers, at every door;
> Old church-yards stuffed with buried crimes,
>   Be clad in sunshine o'er and o'er.—"

"Oh, here!" exclaimed the wretched Bert,
jumping to his feet; "let up on that dismal
recitative. It would make a dog howl to hear
that!"

"Then you 'let up' on that suicidal talk of
marrying," replied John, "and all that ha-
rangue of incoherency about your growing
old. Why, my dear fellow, you 're at least a
dozen years my junior, and look at me!"
and John glanced at himself in the glass with
a feeble pride, noting the gray sparseness of
his side-hair, and its plaintive dearth on top.
"Of course I 've got to admit," he continued,
"that my hair is gradually evaporating; but
for all that, I 'm 'still in the ring,' do n't you
know; as young in society, for the matter of
that, as yourself! And this is just the reason
why I do n't want you to blight every pros-
pect in your life by marrying at your age—
especially a woman—I mean the kind of
woman you 'd be sure to fancy at your age."

"Did n't I say 'a good, sensible girl' was
the kind I had selected?" Bert remonstrated.

"Oh!" exclaimed John, "you've selected her, then?—and without one word to me!" he ended, rebukingly.

"Well, hang it all!" said Bert, impatiently; "I knew how *you* were, and just how you'd talk me out of it; and I made up my mind that for once, at least, I'd follow the dictations of a heart that—however capricious in youthful frivolties—should beat, in manhood, loyal to itself and loyal to its own affinity."

"Go it! Fire away! Farewell, vain world!" exclaimed the excited John.—"Trade your soul off for a pair of ear-bobs and a button-hook—a hank of jute hair and a box of lily-white! I've buried not less than ten old chums this way, and here's another nominated for the tomb."

"But you've got no *reason* about you," began Bert,—"I want to"—

"And so do *I* 'want to,'" broke in John, finally,—"I want to get some sleep.—So 'register' and come to bed.—And lie up on edge, too, when you *do* come—'cause this old catafalque-of-a-bed is just about as narrow as your views of single blessedness! Peace! Not another word! Pile in! Pile in! I'm three-parts sick, anyhow, and I want rest!" And very truly he spoke.

It was a bright morning when the slothful John was aroused by a long, vociferous pounding on the door. He started up in bed to find himself alone—the victim of his wrathful irony having evidently risen and fled away while his pitiless tormentor slept—" Doubtless to at once accomplish that nefarious intent as set forth by his unblushing confession of last night," mused the miserable John. And he ground his fingers in the corners of his swollen eyes, and leered grimly in the glass at the feverish orbs, blood-shotten, blurred and aching.

The pounding on the door continued. John looked at his watch; it was only 8 o'clock.

" Hi, there ! " he called viciously. "What do you mean, anyhow?" he went on, elevating his voice again; " shaking a man out of bed when he's just dropping into his first sleep?"

"I mean that you're going to get up; that's what!" replied a firm female voice. " It's 8 o'clock, and I want to put your room in order; and I'm not going to wait all day about it, either! Get up and go down to your breakfast, and let me have the room!" And the clamor at the door was industriously renewed.

" Say ! " called John, querulously, hurrying on his clothes, " Say ! you ! "

" There's no 'say' about it !" responded

the determined voice : " I 've heard about you and your ways around this house, and I 'm not going to put up with it! You 'll not lie in bed till high noon when I 've got to keep your room in proper order !"

" Oh ho ! " bawled John, intelligently : "reckon you 're the new invasion here? Doubt-less you 're the girl that 's been hanging up the new window-blinds that won't roll, and disguising the pillows with clean slips, and 'hennin' round among my books and papers on the table here, and ageing me generally till I do n't know my own handwriting by the time I find it ! Oh, yes ! you 're going to revolutionize things here ; you 're going to introduce prompt-ness, and system, and order. See you 've even filled the wash-pitcher and tucked two starched towels through the handle. Have n't got any tin towels, have you? I rather like this new soap, too ! So solid and durable, you know ; warranted not to raise a lather. Might as well wash one's hands with a door-knob ! " And as John's voice grumbled away into the sullen silence again, the determined voice without responded : "Oh, you can growl away to your heart's content, Mr. McKinney, but I want you to distinctly understand that I 'm not going to humor you in any of your old bach-elor, sluggardly, slovenly ways, and whims

5

and notions. And I want you to understand, too, that I 'm not hired help in this house, nor a chambermaid, nor anything of the kind. I 'm the landlady here ; and I 'll give you just ten minutes more to get down to your breakfast, or you 'll not get any—that 's all !'" And as the reversed cuff John was in the act of .buttoning slid from his wrist and rolled under the dresser, he heard a stiff rustling of starched muslin flouncing past the door, and the quick italicized patter of determined gaiters down the hall.

"Look here," said John to the bright-faced boy in the hotel office, a half hour later. "It seems the house here 's been changing hands again."

"Yes, sir," said the boy, closing the cigar case, and handing him a lighted match. "Well, the new landlord, whoever he is," continued John, patronizingly, "is a good one. Leastwise, he knows what 's good to eat, and how to serve it."

The boy laughed timidly,—"It aint a 'landlord,' though — it 's a landlady; it 's my mother."

"Ah," said John, dallying with the change the boy had pushed toward him. "Your mother, eh?" And where 's your father?"

"He 's dead," said the boy.

"And what's this for?" abruptly asked John, examining his change.

"That's your change," said the boy: "You got three for a quarter, and gave me a half."

"Well, *you* just keep it," said John, sliding back the change. "It's for good luck, you know, my boy. Same as drinking your long life and prosperity. And, Oh yes, by the way, you may tell your mother I'll have a friend to dinner with me to-day."

"Yes, sir, and thank you, sir," said the beaming boy.

"Handsome boy!" mused John, as he walked down street. "Takes that from his father, though, I'll wager my existence!"

Upon his office desk John found a hastily written note. It was addressed in the well-known hand of his old chum. He eyed the missive apprehensively, and there was a positive pathos in his voice as he said aloud, "It's our divorce. I feel it!" The note, headed, "At the Office, 4 in Morning," ran like this:

"Dear Mack—I left you slumbering so soundly that, by noon, when you waken, I hope, in your refreshed state, you will look more tolerantly on my intentions as partially confided to you this night. I will not see you here again to say good-bye. I wanted to, but

was afraid to 'rouse the sleeping lion.' I will
not close my eyes to-night—fact is, I have n't
time. Our serenade at Josie's was a pre-ar-
ranged signal by which she is to be ready and
at the station for the 5 morning train. You
may remember the lighting of three consecu-
tive matches at her window before the igniting
of her lamp. That meant, 'Thrice dearest one,
I 'll meet thee at the depot at 4 : 30 sharp.'
So, my dear Mack, this is to inform you that,
even as you read, Josie and I have eloped. It
is all the old man's fault, yet I forgive him.
Hope he 'll return the favor. Josie predicts he
will, inside of a week—or two weeks, anyhow.
Good-bye, Mack, old boy; and let a fellow
down as easy as you can. Affectionately,

" BERT."

" Heavens ! " exclaimed John, stifling the
note in his hand and stalking tragically around
the room. " Can it be possible that I have
nursed a frozen viper? An ingrate? A wolf in
sheep's clothing? An orang-outang in gent's
furnishings?"

" Was you callin' me, sir?" asked a voice
at the door. It was the janitor.

"No ! " thundered John; " Quit my sight !
get out of my way ! No, no, Thompson, I do n't
mean that," he called after him. "Here 's a
half dollar for you, and I want you to lock up

the office, and tell anybody that wants to see
me that I've been set upon, and sacked and
assassinated in cold blood; and I've fled to
my father's in the country, and am lying there
in the convulsions of dissolution, babbling of
green fields and running brooks, and thirsting
for the life of every woman that comes in gunshot!" And then, more like a confirmed in-
valid than a man in the strength and pride of
his prime, he crept down into the street again,
and thence back to his hotel.

Dejectedly and painfully climbing to his
room, he encountered, on the landing above,
a little woman in a jaunty dusting-cap and a
trim habit of crisp muslin. He tried to evade
her, but in vain. She looked him squarely in
the face—occasioning him the dubious impres-
sion of either needing shaving very badly, or
having egg-stains on his chin.

"You're the gentleman in No. 11, I believe?" she said.

He nodded confusedly.

"Mr. McKinney is your name, I think?"
she queried, with a pretty elevation of the eye
brows.

"Yes, ma'am," said John, rather abjectly.
"You see, ma'am—But I beg pardon," he
went on stammeringly, and with a very awk-

ward bow—"I beg pardon, but I am addressing—ah—the—ah—the—"

"You are addressing the new landlady,"
she interpolated, pleasantly. "Mrs. Miller
is my name. I think we should be friends,
Mr. McKinney, since I hear that you are one
of the oldest patrons of the house."

"Thank you—thank you!" said John, com-
pletely embarrassed. "Yes, indeed!—ha, ha.
Oh, yes—yes—really, we must be quite old
friends, I assure you, Mrs.—Mrs.—"

"Mrs. Miller," smilingly prompted the little
woman.

"Yes, ah, yes,—Mrs. Miller. Lovely morning, Mrs. Miller," said John, edging past her
and backing toward his room.

But as Mrs. Miller was laughing outright, for
some mysterious reason, and gave no affirma-
tion in response to his proposition as to the
quality of the weather, John, utterly abashed
and nonplussed, darted into his room and
closed the door. "Deucedly extraordinary
woman!" he thought; "wonder what's her
idea!"

He remained locked in his room till the
dinner-hour; and, when he promptly emerged
for that occasion, there was a very noticeable
improvement in his personal appearance, in
point of dress, at least, though there still

lingered about his smoothly-shaven features a certain haggard, care-worn, anxious look that would not out.

Next his own place at the table he found a chair tilted forward, as though in reservation for some honored guest. What did it mean? Oh, he remembered now. Told the boy to tell his mother he would have a friend to dine with him. Bert—and, blast the fellow! he was, doubtless, dining then with a far preferable companion—his wife—in a palace-car on the P., C. & St. L., a hundred miles away. The thought was maddening. Of course, now, the landlady would have material for a new assault. And how could he avert it? A despairing film blurred his sight for the moment—then the eyes flashed daringly. " I will meet it like a man!" he said, mentally— " yea, like a State's Attorney,—I will invite it! Let her do her worst!"

He called a servant, directing some message in an undertone.

" Yes, sir," said the agreeable servant, "I 'll go right away, sir," and left the room.

Five minutes elapsed, and then a voice at his shoulder startled him:

" Did you send for me, Mr. McKinney? What is it I can do?"

" You are very kind. Mrs.— Mrs.—"

"Mrs. Miller," said the lady, with a smile that he remembered.

"Now, please spare me even the mildest of rebukes. I deserve your censure, but I can't stand it—I can't positively!" and there was a pleading look in John's lifted eyes that changed the little woman's smile to an expression of real solicitude. "I have sent for you," continued John, "to ask of you three great favors. Please be seated while I enumerate them. First—I want you to forgive and forget that ill-natured, uncalled-for grumbling of mine this morning when you wakened me."

"Why, certainly," said the landlady, again smiling, though quite seriously.

"I thank you," said John, with dignity. "And, second," he continued—"I want your assurance that my extreme confusion and awkwardness on the occasion of our meeting later were rightly interpreted."

"Certainly—certainly," said the landlady, with the kindliest sympathy.

"I am grateful—utterly," said John, with newer dignity. "And then," he went on,— "after informing you that it is impossible for the best friend I have in the world to be with me at this hour, as intended, I want you to do me the very great honor of dining with me. Will you?"

"Why, certainly," said the charming little landlady—"and a thousand thanks beside! But tell me something of your friend," she continued, as they were being served. "What is he like—and what is his name—and where is he?"

"Well," said John, warily,—"he's like all young fellows of his age. He's quite young, you know—not over thirty, I should say—a mere boy, in fact, but clever—talented—versatile."

"—Unmarried, of course," said the chatty little woman.

"Oh, yes!" said John, in a matter-of-course tone—but he caught himself abruptly—then stared intently at his napkin—glanced evasively at the side-face of his questioner, and said,—"Oh yes! Yes, indeed! He's unmarried.—Old bachelor like myself, you know. Ha! Ha!"

"So he's not like the young man here that distinguished himself last night?" said the little woman, archly.

The fork in John's hand, half-lifted to his lips, faltered and fell back toward his plate.

"Why, what's that?" said John, in a strange voice; "I hadn't heard anything about it—I mean I haven't heard anything about any young man. What was it?"

"Have n't heard anything about the elopement?" exclaimed the little woman, in as-
tonishment.—"Why, it 's been the talk of
the town all morning. Elopement in high
life—son of a grain-dealer, name of Hines,
or Himes, or something, and a preacher's
daughter—Josie somebody—did n't catch her
last name. Wonder if you do n't know the
parties—Why, Mr. McKinney, are you ill?"

"Oh, no—not at all!" said John: "Do n't
mention it. Ha—ha! Just eating too rapidly,
that 's all. Go on with—you were saying that
Bert and Josie had really eloped."

"What 'Bert'?" asked the little woman
quickly.

"Why, did I say Bert?" said John, with a
guilty look. "I meant Haines, of course, you
know—Haines and Josie.—And did they really
elope?"

"That 's the report," answered the little
woman, as though deliberating some important evidence; "and they say, too, that the
plot of the runaway was quite ingenious. It
seems the young lovers were assisted in their
flight by some old fellow—friend of the young
man's——Why, Mr. McKinney, you *are* ill,
surely?"

John's face was ashen.

"No—no!" he gasped, painfully: "Go

on—go on! Tell me more about the—the—
the old fellow—the old reprobate! And is he
still at large?"

"Yes," said the little womon, anxiously
regarding the strange demeanor of her companion. "They say, though, that the law can
do nothing with him, and that this fact only
intensifies the agony of the broken-hearted
parents—for it seems they have, till now, re-
garded him both as a gentleman and family
friend in whom "—

" I really am ill," moaned John, waveringly
rising to his feet; "but I beg you not to be
alarmed. Tell your little boy to come to my
room, where I will retire at once, if you 'll
excuse me, and send for my physician. It is
simply a nervous attack. I am often troubled
so; and only perfect quiet and seclusion re-
stores me. You have done me a great honor,
Mrs."—(" Mrs.—Miller," sighed the sympa-
thetic little woman)—" Mrs. Miller,—and I
thank you more than I have words to express."
He bowed limply, turned through a side door
opening on a stair, and tottered to his room.

During the three weeks' illness through
which he passed, John had every attention—
much more, indeed, than he had conscious-
ness to appreciate. For the most part his

mind wandered, and he talked of curious things, and laughed hysterically, and serenaded mermaids that dwelt in grassy seas of dew, and were bald-headed like himself. He played upon a fourteen-jointed flute of solid gold, with diamond holes, and keys carved out of thawless ice. His old father came at first to take him home; but he could not be moved, the doctor said.

Two weeks of John's illness had worn away, when a very serious looking young man, in a traveling duster, and a high hat, came up the stairs to see him. A handsome young lady was clinging to his arm. It was Bert and Josie. She had guessed the very date of their forgiveness. John wakened even clearer in mind than usual that afternoon. He recognized his old chum at a glance, and Josie— now Bert's wife. Yes, he comprehended that. He was holding a hand of each when another figure entered. His thin, white fingers loosened their clasp, and he held a hand toward the new comer. "Here," he said, " is my best friend in the world—Bert, you and Josie will love her, I know; for this is Mrs.—Mrs."— "Mrs. Miller," said the radiant little woman.— "Yes,—Mrs. Miller," said John, very proudly.

Rhymes of Rainy Days

THE TREE-TOAD.

"'SCURIOUS-LIKE," said the tree-toad,
    "I've twittered fer rain all day;
        And I got up soon,
        And I hollered till noon—
    But the sun, hit blazed away,
        Till I jest clumb down in a crawfish-hole,
        Weary at heart, and sick at soul!

"Dozed away fer an hour,
    And I tackled the thing agin;
        And I sung, and sung,
        Till I knowed my lung
    Was jest about give in;
        And then, thinks I, ef hit do n't rain now,
        There 're nothin' in singin', anyhow!

"Once in awhile some
    Would come a drivin' past;
        And he'd hear my cry,
        And stop and sigh—
    Till I jest laid back, at last,
        And I hollered rain till I thought my th'oat
        Would bust right open at ever' note!

"But I *fetched* her! O *I fetched* her!—
    'Cause a little while ago,
        As I kindo' set,
        With one eye shet,
    And a-singin' soft and low,
        A voice drapped down on my fevered brain,
        Sayin',—'Ef you'll jest hush I'll rain!'"

(79)

A WORN-OUT PENCIL.

WELLADAY!
Here I lay
You at rest—all worn away,
    O my pencil, to the tip
    Of our old companionship!

Memory
Sighs to see
What you are, and used to be,
    Looking backward to the time
    When you wrote your earliest rhyme!—

When I sat
Filing at
Your first point, and dreaming that
    Your initial song should be
    Worthy of posterity.

With regret
I forget
If the song be living yet,
    Yet remember, vaguely now,
    It was honest, anyhow.

You have brought
Me a thought—
Truer yet was never taught,—
    That the silent song is best,
    And the unsung worthiest.

(80)

So if I,
When I die,
May as uncomplainingly
    Drop aside as now you do,
    Write of me, as I of you:—

Here lies one
Who begun
Life a-singing, heard of none;
    And he died, satisfied,
    With his dead songs by his side.

6

THE STEPMOTHER.

FIRST she come to our house,
  Tommy run and hid;
And Emily and Bob and me
  We cried jus' like we did
When Mother died,—and we all said
'At we all wisht 'at we was dead!

And Nurse she could n't stop us,
  And Pa he tried and tried,—
We sobbed and shook and would n't look,
  But only cried and cried;
And nen someone—we could n't jus'
Tell who—was cryin' same as us!

Our Stepmother! Yes, it was her,
  Her arms around us all—
'Cause Tom slid down the bannister
  And peeked in from the hall.—
And we all love her, too, because
She 's purt nigh good as Mother was!

THE RAIN.

I.

THE RAIN! the rain! the rain!
  It gushed from the skies and streamed
Like awful tears; and the sick man thought
  How pitiful it seemed!
And he turned his face away,
  And stared at the wall again,
His hopes nigh dead and his heart worn out.
  O the rain! the rain! the rain!

II.

The rain! the rain! the rain!
  And the broad stream brimmed the shores;
And ever the river crept over the reeds
  And the roots of the sycamores:
A corpse swirled by in a drift
  Where the boat had snapt its chain—
And a hoarse-voiced mother shrieked and raved.
  O the rain! the rain! the rain!

III.

The rain! the rain! the rain!—
  Pouring, with never a pause,
Over the fields and the green byways—
  How beautiful it was!
And the new-made man and wife
  Stood at the window-pane
Like two glad children kept from school.—
  O the rain! the rain! the rain!

THE LEGEND GLORIFIED.

"I DEEM that God is not disquieted "—
This in a mighty poet's rhymes I read;
And blazoned so forever doth abide
Within my soul the legend glorified.

Though awful tempests thunder overhead,
I deem that God is not disquieted,—
The faith that trembles somewhat yet is sure
Through storm and darkness of a way secure.

Bleak winters, when the naked spirit hears
The break of hearts, through stinging sleet of tears,
I deem that God is not disquieted;
Against all stresses am I clothed and fed.

Nay, even with fixed eyes and broken breath,
My feet dip down into the tides of death,
Nor any friend be left, nor prayer be said,
I deem that God is not disquieted.

WANT TO BE WHUR MOTHER IS.

"WANT TO BE whur mother is! Want to be whur
mother is!"
Jeemses Rivers! wo n't some one ever shet that howl o' his?
That-air yellin' drives me wild!
Cain 't none of ye stop the child?
Want yer Daddy? "Naw." Gee whizz!
" Want to be whur mother is!"

"Want to be whur mother is! Want to be whur mother is!"
Coax him, Sairy! Mary, sing somepin fer him! Lift him,
Liz—
Bang the clock-bell with the key—
Er the *meat-ax!* Gee-mun-nee!
Listen to them lungs o' his!
" Want to be whur mother is!"

"Want to be whur mother is! Want to be whur mother is!"
Preacher guess 'll pound all night on that old pulpit o' his;
'Pears to me some wimmin jest
Shows religious interest
Mostly 'fore their fambly 's riz!
" Want to be whur mother is!"

* * * * * * * *

"Want to be whur mother is! Want to be whur mother is!"
Nights like these and whipperwills allus brings that voice
of his!
Sairy; Mary; 'Lizabeth;
Do n't set there and ketch yer **death**
In the dew—er rheumatiz—
Want to be whur mother is?

(85)

OLD MAN'S NURSERY RHYME.

I.

IN THE jolly winters
  Of the long-ago,
It was not so cold as now—
  O! No! No!
Then, as I remember,
  Snowballs, to eat,
Were as good as apples now,
  And every bit as sweet!

II.

In the jolly winters
  Of the dead-and-gone,
Bub was warm as summer,
  With his red mitts on,—
Just in his little waist-
  And-pants all together,
Who ever heard him growl
  About cold weather?

III.

In the jolly winters of the long-ago—
Was it *half* so cold as now?
  O! No! No!
Who caught his death o' cold,
  Making prints of men
Flat-backed in snow that now's
  Twice as cold again?

IV.

In the jolly winters
  Of the dead-and-gone,
Startin' out rabbit-hunting
  Early as the dawn,—
Who ever froze his fingers,
  Ears, heels, or toes,—
Or 'd a cared if he had?
  Nobody knows!

V.

Nights by the kitchen-stove,
  Shelling white and red
Corn in the skillet, and
  Sleepin' four abed!
Ah! the jolly winters
  Of the long-ago!
We were not so old as now—
  O! No! No!

THREE DEAD FRIENDS.

ALWAYS suddenly they are gone—
 The friends we trusted and held secure—
 Suddenly we are gazing on,
 Not a *smiling* face, but the marble-pure
Dead mask of a face that nevermore
 To a smile of ours will make reply—
  The lips close-locked as the eyelids are.—
Gone—swift as the flash of the molten ore
 A meteor pours through a midnight sky,
  Leaving it blind of a single star.

Tell us, O Death, Remorseless Might!
 What is this old, unescapable ire
You wreak on us?—from the birth of light
 Till the world be charred to a core of fire!
We do no evil thing to you—
 We seek to evade you—that is all—
  That is your will—you will not be known
Of men. What, then, would you have us do?—
 Cringe, and wait till your vengeance fall,
  And your graves be fed, and the trumpet blown?

You desire no friends; but *we*—O we
 Need them so, as we falter here,
Fumbling through each new vacancy,
 As each is stricken that we hold dear.
One you struck but a year ago;
 And one not a month ago; and one—
  (God's vast pity!)—and one lies now
Where the widow wails, in her nameless woe,
 And the soldiers pace, with the sword and gun,
  Where the comrade sleeps, with the laureled brow.

(88)

And what did the first?—that wayward soul,
 Clothed of sorrow, yet nude of sin,
And with all hearts bowed in the strange control
 Of the heavenly voice of his violin.
Why, it was music the way he *stood*,
 So grand was the poise of the head and so
 Full was the figure of majesty!—
One heard with the eyes, as a deaf man would,
 And with all sense brimmed to the overflow
 With tears of anguish and ecstasy.

And what did the girl, with the great warm light
 Of genius sunning her eyes of blue,
With her heart so pure, and her soul so white—
 What, O Death, did she do to you?
Through field and wood as a child she strayed,
 As Nature, the dear sweet mother led;
 While from her canvas, mirrored back,
Glimmered the stream through the everglade
 Where the grapevine trailed from the trees to wed
 Its likeness of emerald, blue and black.

And what did he, who, the last of these,
 Faced you, with never a fear, O Death?
Did you hate *him* that he loved the breeze,
 And the morning dews, and the rose's breath?
Did you hate him that he answered not
 Your hate again—but turned, instead,
 His only hate on his country's wrongs?
Well—you possess him, dead!—but what
 Of the good he wrought?   With laureled head
 He bides with us in his deeds and songs.

Laureled, first, that he bravely fought,
 And forged a way to our flag's release;
Laureled, next—for the harp he taught
 To wake glad songs in the days of peace—
Songs of the woodland haunts he held

As close in his love as they held their bloom
   In their inmost bosoms of leaf and vine—
Songs that echoed, and pulsed and welled
    Through the town's pent streets, and the sick child's
      room,
     Pure as a shower in soft sunshine.

Claim them, Death; yet their fame endures,
   What friend next will you rend from us
In that cold, pitiless way of yours,
    And leave us a grief more dolorous?
Speak to us!—tell us, O Dreadful Power!—
    Are we to have not a lone friend left?—
      Since, frozen, sodden, or green the sod,—
In every second of every hour,
    Some one, Death, you have left thus bereft,
     Half inaudibly shrieks to God.

IN BOHEMIA.

HA! MY DEAR! I'm back again—
Vendor of Bohemia's wares!
Lordy! How it pants a man
Climbing up those awful stairs!
Well, I've made the dealer say
Your sketch *might* sell, anyway!
And I've made a publisher
Hear my poem, Kate, my dear.

In Bohemia, Kate, my dear—
Lodgers in a musty flat
On the top floor—living here
Neighborless, and used to that,—
Like a nest beneath the eaves,
So our little home receives
Only guests of chirping cheer—
We'll be happy, Kate, my dear!

Under your north-light there, you
At your easel, with a stain
On your nose of Prussian blue,
Paint your bits of shine and rain;
With my feet thrown up at will
O'er my littered window-sill,
I write rhymes that ring as clear
As your laughter, Kate, my dear.

Puff my pipe, and stroke my hair—
Bite my pencil-tip and gaze
At you, mutely mooning there
O'er your "Aprils" and your "Mays!"

(91)

Equal inspiration in
Dimples of your cheek and chin,
And the golden atmosphere
Of your paintings, Kate, my dear!

Trying! Yes, at times it is,
  To clink happy rhymes, and fling
On the canvas scenes of bliss,
  When we are half famishing!—
    When your "jersey" rips in spots,
    And your hat's "forget-me-nots"
    Have grown tousled, old and sere—
    It is trying, Kate, my dear!

But—as sure—*some* picture sells,
  And—sometimes—the poetry—
Bless us! How the parrot yells
  His acclaims at you and me!
    How we revel then in scenes
    Of high banqueting!—sardines—
    Salads—olives—and a sheer
    Pint of sherry, Kate, my dear!

Even now I cross your palm,
  With this great round world of gold!—
"Talking wild?" Perhaps I am—
  Then, this little five-year-old!—
    Call it anything you will,
    So it lifts your face until
    I may kiss away that tear
    Ere it drowns me, Kate, my dear.

IN THE DARK.

O IN THE depths of midnight
　　What fancies haunt the brain!
When even the sigh of the sleeper
　　Sounds like a sob of pain.

A sense of awe and of wonder
　　I may never well define,—
For the thoughts that come in the shadows
　　Never come in the shine.

The old clock down in the parlor
　　Like a sleepless mourner grieves,
And the seconds drip in the silence
　　As the rain drips from the eaves.

And I think of the hands that signal
　　The hours there in the gloom,
And wonder what angel watchers
　　Wait in the darkened room.

And I think of the smiling faces
　　That used to watch and wait,
Till the click of the clock was answered
　　By the click of the opening gate.—

They are not there now in the evening—
　　Morning or noon—not there;
Yet I know that they keep their vigil,
　　And wait for me Somewhere.

(93)

WET WEATHER TALK.

IT AIN'T no use to grumble and complain;
It's jest as cheap and easy to rejoice:
When God sorts out the weather and sends rain,
W'y, rain's my choice.

Men giner'ly, to all intents—
Although they're ap' to grumble some—
Puts most their trust in Providence,
And takes things as they come;—
That is, the commonality
Of men that's lived as long as me,
Has watched the world enough to learn
They're not the boss of the concern.

With *some*, of course, it's different—
I've seed *young* men that knowed it all,
And did n't like the way things went
On this terrestial ball!
But, all the same, the rain some way
Rained jest as hard on picnic-day;
Er when they railly wanted it,
It maybe would n't rain a bit!

In this existence, dry and wet
Will overtake the best of men—
Some little skift o' clouds 'll shet
The sun off now and then;
But maybe, while you 're wondern' who
You 've fool-like lent your umbrell' to,
And *want* it—out 'll pop the sun,
And you 'll be glad you ain't got none!

)

It aggervates the farmers, too—
  They 's too much wet, er too much sun,
Er work, er waiting round to do
  Before the plowin' 's done;
    And maybe, like as not, the wheat,
    Jest as it 's lookin' hard to beat,
    Will ketch the storm—and jest about
    The time the corn 's a-jintin' out!

These here cy-clones a-foolin' round—
  And back'ard crops—and wind and rain,
And yit the corn that 's wallered down
  May elbow up again!
    They ain't no sense, as I kin see,
    In mortals, sich as you and me,
    A-faultin' Nature's wise intents,
    And lockin' horns with Providence!

It ain't no use to grumble and complain;
  It 's jest as cheap and easy to rejoice:
When God sorts out the weather and sends rain,
    W'y, rain 's my choice.

WHERE SHALL WE LAND.

"Where shall we land you, sweet?"—Swinburne

ALL LISTLESSLY we float
    Out seaward in the boat
      That beareth Love.
Our sails of purest snow
Bend to the blue below
      And to the blue above.
          Where shall we land?

We drift upon a tide
Shoreless on every side,
      Save where the eye
Of Fancy sweeps far lands
Shelved slopingly with sands
      Of gold and porphyry.
          Where shall we land?

The fairy isles we see,
Loom up so mistily—
      So vaguely fair,
We do not care to break
Fresh bubbles in our wake
      To bend our course for there.
          Where shall we land?

The warm winds of the deep
Have lulled our sails to sleep,
      And so we glide
Careless of wave or wind,
Or change of any kind,
      Or turn of any tide.
          Where shall we land?

(96)

We droop our dreamy eyes
Where our reflection lies
    Steeped in the sea,
And, in an endless fit
Of languor, smile on it
    And its sweet mimicry.
        Where shall we land?

"Where shall we land?" God's grace!
I know not any place
    So fair as this—
Swung here between the blue
Of sea and sky, with you
    To ask me, with a kiss,
        "Where shall we land?"

7

Champion Checker-Player
of Ameriky

THE CHAMPION CHECKER-PLAYER OF AMERIKY.

OF course as fur as Checker-playin's concerned, you can't jest adzackly claim
'at lots makes fortunes and lots gits bu'sted at it
—but still, it's on'y simple jestice to acknowl-
edge 'at there're absolute p'ints in the game 'at
takes scientific principles to figger out, and a
mighty level-headed feller to *dim*onstrate, don't
you understand!

Checkers is a' *old* enough game, ef age is any
rickommendation; and it's a' evident fact, too,
'at "the tooth of time," as the feller says, which
fer the last six thousand years has gained some
reputation fer a-eatin' up things in giner'l, don't
'pear to 'a' gnawed much of a hole in Checkers
—jedgin' from the checker-board of to-day and
the ones 'at they're uccasionally shovellin' out
at *Pom*p'y-*i*, er whatever its name is.   Turned
up a checker-board there not long ago, I wuz
readin' 'bout, 'at still had the spots on—as
plain and fresh as the modern white-pine board
o' our'n, squared off with pencil-marks and

pokeberry-juice.   These is facts 'at history her-
self has dug out, and of course it ain't fer me
ner you to turn our nose up at Checkers, whuther
we ever tamper with the fool-game er not. Fur's
that's concerned, I don't p'tend to be no checker-player *myse'f*,—but I know'd a feller onc't
'at *could* play, and sorto' made a business of it;
and *that* man, in my opinion, was a geenyus!
Name wuz Wesley Cotterl—John Wesley Cotterl—jest plain Wes, as us fellers round the
Shoe-Shop ust to call him; ust to allus make
the Shoe-Shop his headquarters-like; and, rain
er shine, wet er dry, you'd allus find *Wes* on
hands, ready to banter some feller fer a game,
er jest a-settin' humped up there over the checker-board all alone, a-cipher'n' out some new
move er 'nuther, and whistlin' low and solem'
to hisse'f-like and a-payin' no attention to nobody.

And *I'll* tell *you*, Wes Cotterl wuz no man's
fool, as sly as you keep it! He wuz a deep
thinker, Wes wuz; and ef he'd 'a' jest turned
that mind o' his loose on *preachin'*, fer instunce,
and the 'terpertation o' the Bible, don't you
know, Wes 'ud 'a' worked p'ints out o' there
'at no livin' expounderers ever got in gunshot of!

But Wes he didn't 'pear to be cut out fer
nothin' much but jest Checker-playin'. Oh, of

course, he *could* knock round his own woodpile
some, and garden a little, more er less; and the
neighbers ust to find Wes purty handy 'bout
trimmin' fruit-trees, you understand, and work-
in' in among the worms and cattapillers in the
vines and shrubbery, and the like.   And handlin' bees!—They wuzn't no man under the
heavens 'at knowed more 'bout handlin' bees'n
Wes Cotterl!—"Settlin'" the blame' things
when they wuz a-swarmin'; and a-robbin' hives,
and all sich fool-resks.   W'y, I've saw Wes Cotterl, 'fore now, when a swarm of bees 'ud settle
in a' orchard,—like they will sometimes, you
know,—I've saw Wes Cotterl jest roll up his
shirt-sleeves and bend down a' apple tree limb
'at wuz jest kivvered with the pesky things, and
scrape 'em back into the hive with his naked
hands, by the quart and gallon, and never git a
scratch!   You couldn't *hire* a bee to sting Wes
Cotterl!   But *lazy?*—I think that man had
railly ort to 'a' been a' Injun!   He wuz the fust
and on'y man 'at ever I laid eyes on 'at wuz too
lazy to drap a checker-man to p'int out the
right road fer a feller 'at ast him onc't the way
to Burke's Mill; and Wes, 'ithout ever a-liftin'
eye er finger, jest sorto' crooked out that mouth
o' his'n in the direction the feller wanted, and
says: *"H-yonder!"* and went on with his whist-

lin'. But all this hain't Checkers, and that's
what I started out to tell ye.

Wes had a way o' jest natchurly a-cleanin'
out anybody and ever'body 'at 'ud he'p
hold up a checker-board! Wes wuzn't what
you'd call a *lively* player at all, ner a competiter 'at talked much 'crost the board er made
much furse over a game whilse he *wuz* a-playin'. He had his faults, o' course, and *would*
take back moves 'casion'ly, er inch up on you
ef you didn't watch him, mebby. But, *as a
rule*, Wes had the insight to grasp the idy of
whoever wuz a-playin' ag'in' him, and *his* style
o' game, you understand, and wuz on the look-
out continual'; and under sich circumstances
could play as *honest* a game o' Checkers as the
babe unborn.

One thing in *Wes's* favor allus wuz the feller's
temper.—Nothin' 'peared to aggervate Wes,
and nothin' on earth could break his slow and
lazy way o' takin' his own time fer ever'thing.
You jest *couldn't crowd Wes* er git him rattled
anyway.—Jest 'peared to have one fixed princi-
ple, and that wuz to take plenty o' time, and
never make no move 'ithout a-ciphern'n' ahead
on the prob'ble consequences, don't you understand! ''Be shore you're right,'' Wes 'ud say,
a-lettin' up fer a second on that low and sorry-

like little wind-through-the-keyhole whistle o'
his, and a-nosin' out a place whur he could swap
one man fer two.—"Be shore you're right"—
and somep'n' after this style wuz Wes's way: "Be
shore you're right"—(whistling a long, lonesome bar of "Barbara Allen")—"and then"—
(another long, retarded bar)—"go ahead!"—
and by the time the feller 'ud git through with his
whistlin', and a-stoppin' and a-startin' in ag'in,
he'd be about three men ahead to your one.
And then he'd jest go on with his whistlin'
'sef nothin' had happened, and mebby you
a-jest a-rearin' and a-callin' him all the mean,
outlandish, ornry names 'at you could lay
tongue to.

But Wes's good nature, I reckon, was the
thing 'at he'ped him out as much as any other
p'ints the feller had. And *Wes 'ud allus win,
in the long run!*—I don't keer *who* played
ag'inst him! It was on'y a question o' time
with Wes o' waxin' it to the best of 'em. Lots
o' players has *tackled* Wes, and right at the
start 'ud mebby give him trouble,—but in the
long run, now mind ye—*in the long run*, no
mortal man, I reckon, had any business o' rub-
bin' knees with Wes Cotterl under no airthly
checker-board in all this vale o' tears!

I mind onc't th' come along a high-toned

feller from in around In'i'nop'lus somers.—Wuz
a *lawyer*, er some *p'fessional* kind o' man.
Had a big yaller, luther-kivvered book under
his arm, and a bunch o' these-'ere big en*vel*op's
and a lot o' suppeenies stickin' out o' his breast-
pocket.   Mighty slick-lookin' feller he wuz;
wore a stove-pipe hat, sorto' set 'way back on
his head—so's to show off his Giner'l Jackson
forr'ed, don't you know!   Well-sir, this feller
struck the place, on some business er other, and
then missed the hack 'at *ort* to 'a' tuk him out
o' here sooner'n it *did* take him out!—And
whilse he wuz a-loafin' round, sorto' lonesome—
like a feller allus *is* in a strange place, you know
—he kindo' drapped in on our crowd at the
Shoe-Shop, ostenchably to git a boot-strop
stitched on, but *I* knowed, the minute he set
foot in the door, 'at *that* feller wanted *comp'ny*
wuss'n *cobblin'*.

Well, as good luck would have it, there set
Wes, as usual, with the checker-board in his
lap, a-playin' all by hisse'f, and a-whistlin' so
low and solem'-like and sad it railly made the
crowd seem like a *religious* getherun' o' some
kind er other, we wuz all so quiet and still-like,
as the man come in.

Well, the stranger stated his business, set
down, tuk off his boot, and set there nussin' his

foot and talkin' weather fer ten minutes, I
reckon, 'fore he ever 'peared to notice Wes at
all. We wuz all back'ard, anyhow, 'bout
talkin' much; besides, we knowed, long afore
he come in, all about how hot the weather wuz,
and the pore chance there wuz o' rain, and all
that; and so the subject had purty well died out,
when jest then the feller's eyes struck Wes and
the checker-board,—and I'll never fergit the
warm, salvation smile 'at flashed over him 'at
the promisin' discovery. "*What!*" says he,
a-grinnin' like a' angel and a-edgin' his cheer
to'rds Wes, "have we a checker-board and
checkers here?"

"We hev," says I, knowin' 'at Wes wouldn't
let go 'o that whistle long enough to answer—
more'n to mebby nod his head.

"And who is your best player?" says the
feller, kindo' pitiful-like, with another inquirin'
look atWes.

"Him," says I, a-pokin' Wes with a peg-
float. But Wes on'y spit kindo' absent-like,
and went on with his whistlin'.

"Much of a player, is he?" says the feller,
with a sorto' doubtful smile at Wes ag'in.

"Plays a purty good hick'ry," says I,
a-pokin' Wes ag'in. "Wes," says I, "here's
a gentleman 'at 'ud mebby like to take a hand

with you there, and give you a few idys,"
says I.

"Yes," says the stranger, eager-like, a-settin'
his plug-hat keerful' up in the empty shelvin',
and a-rubbin' his hands and smilin' as confident-
like as old Hoyle hisse'f,—"Yes, indeed, I'd
be glad to give the gentleman" (meanin' Wes)
"a' idy er two about Checkers—ef *he'd* jest as
lief,—'cause I reckon ef there're any one thing
'at I *do* know more about 'an another, it's
Checkers," says he; "and there're no game 'at
delights me more—*pervidin'*, o' course, I find
a competiter 'at kin make it anyways in-
te*rest*in'."

"Got much of a rickord on Checkers?"
says I.

"Well," says the feller, "I don't like to brag,
but I've never *ben* beat—in any *legitimut* con-
test," says he, "and I've played more'n one o'
them," he says, "here and there round the
country. Of course, *your friend* here," he
went on, smilin' sociable at Wes, "*he'll* take it
all in good part ef I should happen to lead him
a little—jest as *I'd* do," he says, "ef it wuz
possible fer him to lead *me*."

"*Wes*," says I, "*has* warmed the wax in the
yeers of some mighty good checker-players,"
says I, as he squared the board around, still a-

whistlin' to hisse'f-like, as the stranger tuk his place, a-smilin'-like and roachin' back his hair.

"Move," says Wes.

"No," says the feller, with a polite flourish of his hand; "the first move shall be your'n." And, by jucks! fer all he wouldn't take even the advantage of a starter, he flaxed it to Wes the fust game in less'n fifteen minutes.

"Right shore you've give' me your best player?" he says, smilin' round at the crowd, as Wes set squarin' the board fer another game and whistlin' as onconcerned-like as ef nothin' had happened more'n ordinary.

"'S your move," says Wes, a-squintin' out into the game 'bout forty foot from shore, and a-whistlin' purt' nigh in a whisper.

Well-sir, it 'peared-like the feller railly didn't *try* to play; and you could see, too, 'at Wes knowed he'd about met his match, and played accordin'. He didn't make no move at all 'at he didn't give keerful thought to; whilse the feller—! well, as I wuz sayin', it jest 'peared-like *Checkers* wuz *child's-play* fer him! Putt in most o' the time 'long through the game a-sayin' things calkilated to kindo' bore a' ordinary man. But Wes helt hisse'f purty level, and didn't show no signs, and kep' up his *whistlin'*, mighty well—considerin'.

"Reckon you play the *fiddle*, too, as well as *Checkers?*" says the feller, laughin', as Wes come a-whistlin' out of the little end of the second game and went on a-fixin' fer the next round.

"'S my move!" says Wes, 'thout seemin' to notice the feller's tantalizin' words whatsomever.

"'L! *this* time," thinks I, "Mr. Smarty from the *metrolopin* deestricts, *you're* liable to git *waxed—shore!*" But the *feller* didn't 'pear to think so at all, and played right ahead as glib-like and keerless as ever—'casion'ly a-throwin' in them sircastic remarks o' his'n,— 'bout bein' "slow and shore" 'bout things in gineral—"Liked to *see* that," he said:—"Liked to see fellers do things with plenty o' *delibera-tion*, and even ef a feller *wuzn't* much of a checker-player, liked to see him *die* slow *any-how!*—and then 'tend his own funeral," he says,—"and march in the p'session—to his own *music*," says he.—And jest then his remarks wuz brung to a close by Wes a-jumpin' two men, and a-lightin square in the king-row. . . .

"Crown that," says Wes, a-droppin' back into his old tune. And fer the rest o' *that* game Wes helt the feller purty level, but had to finally knock under—but by jest the clos'test kind o' shave o' winnin'.

"They ain't much use," says the feller, "o' keepin' *this* thing up—'less I could manage, *some* way er other, to git beat *onc't 'n a while!*"

"Move," says Wes, a-drappin' back into the same old whistle and a-*settlin'* there.

" 'Music has charms,' as the Good Book tells us," says the feller, kindo' nervous-like, and a-roachin' his hair back as ef some sort o' p'tracted headache wuz a-settin' in.

"Never wuz '*skunked*,' wuz ye?" says Wes, kindo' suddent-like, with a fur-off look in them big white eyes o' his—and then a-whistlin' right on, 'sef he hadn't said *nothin'*.

"*Not much!*" says the feller, sorto' s'prised-like, as ef such a' idy as that had never struck him afore.—"Never was 'skunked' *myse'f:* but I've saw fellers in my time 'at *wuz!*" says he.

But from that time on I noticed the feller 'peared to play more keerful, and railly la'nched into the game with somepin' like inter'st. Wes he seemed to be jest a-limberin'-up-like; and-sir, blame me! ef he didn't walk the feller's log fer him *that* time, 'thout no 'pearent trouble at all!

"And, *now*," says Wes, all quiet-like, a-squar-in' the board fer another'n,—"we're kindo' git-tin' at things *right*. Move." And away went that little unconcerned whistle o' his ag'in, and

Mr. Cityman jest gittin' white and sweaty too—
he wuz so nervous. Ner he didn't 'pear to find
much to laugh at in the *next* game—ner the next
two games nuther! Things wuz a-gettin' mighty
inter*est*in' 'bout them times, and I guess the
feller wuz ser'ous-like a-wakin' up to the solem'
fact 'at it tuk 'bout all *his* spare time to keep
up his end o' the row, and even that state o'
'pore satisfaction wuz a-creepin' furder and furder away from him ever' new turn he undertook.
Whilse *Wes* jest 'peared to git more deliber't'
and certain ever' game; and that unendin' se'f-
satisfied and comfortin' little whistle o' his never
drapped a stitch, but toed out ever' game
alike,—to'rds the *last*, and, fer the *most* part,
disasterss to the feller 'at had started in with sich
confi*dence* and actchul promise, don't you know.

Well-sir, the feller stuck the whole *forenoon*
out, and then the *afternoon;* and then knuckled
down to it 'way into the night—yes, and plum
midnight!—And he buckled into the thing
bright and airly *next morning!* And-sir, fer *two
long days* and nights, a-hardly a-stoppin' long
enough to *eat*, the feller stuck it out,—and Wes
a-jest a-warpin' it to him hand-over-fist, and
leavin' him furder behind, ever' game!—till
finally, to'rds the last, the feller got so blame-
don worked up and excited-like, he jes 'peared

actchully purt' nigh plum crazy and histurical
as a woman!

It wuz a-gittin' late into the shank of the second day, and the boys hed jest lit a candle fer
'em to finish out one of the clost'est games the
feller'd played Wes fer some time.   But Wes
wuz jest as cool and ca'm as ever, and still
a-whistlin' consolin' to hisse'f-like, whilse the
feller jest 'peared wore out and ready to drap
right in his tracks any minute.

"*Durn you!*" he snarled out at Wes, "hain't
you never goern to move?"   And there set Wes,
a-balancin' a checker-man above the board,
a-studyin' whur to set it, and a-fillin' in the
time with that-air whistle.

"*Flames and flashes!*" says the feller ag'in,
"will you *ever* stop that death-seducin' tune o'
your'n long enough to move?"—And as Wes
deliber't'ly set his man down whur the feller see
he'd haf to jump it and lose two men and a king,
Wes wuz a-singin', low and sad-like, as ef all to
hisse'f:

"*O we'll move that man, and leave him there.—
Fer the love of B-a-r-b—bry Al-len!*"

Well-sir! the feller jest jumped to his feet,
upset the board, and tore out o' the shop stark-
starin' crazy—blame ef he wuzn't!—'cause

some of us putt out after him and overtook him 'way beyent the 'pike-bridge, and hollered to him;—and he shuk his fist at us and hollered back and says, says he: "Ef you fellers over here," says he, " 'll agree to *muzzle* that durn checker-player o' your'n, I'll bet fifteen hunderd dollars to fifteen cents 'at I kin beat him 'leven games out of ever' dozent!—But there're *no money*," he says, " 'at kin hire me to play him ag'in, on this aboundin' airth, on'y on them conditions—'cause that durn, eternal, infernal, dad-blasted whistle o' his 'ud beat the oldest man in Ameriky!"

MARTHY ELLEN.

THEY 'S NOTHIN' in the name to strike
A feller more 'n common like!
'Taint liable to git no praise
Ner nothin' like it nowadays;
An' yit that name o' her'n is jest
As purty as the purtiest—
And more 'n that, I 'm here to say
I 'll live a-thinkin' thataway
        And die fer Marthy Ellen!

It may be I was prejudust
In favor of it from the fust—
'Cause I kin ricollect jest how
We met, and hear her mother now
A-callin' of her down the road—
And, aggervatin' little toad!—
I see her now, jes' sort o' half-
Way disapp'inted, turn and laugh
        And mock her—" Marthy Ellen!"

Our people never had no fuss,
And yit they never tuck to us;
We neighbered back and foreds some;
Until they see she liked to come
To our house—and me and her
Were jest together ever'whur
And all the time—and when they 'd see
That I liked her and she liked me,
        They 'd holler "Marthy Ellen!"

(119)

When we growed up, and they shet down
On me and her a-runnin' roun'
Together, and her father said
He'd never leave her nary red,
So he'p him, ef she married me,
And so on—and her mother she
Jest agged the gyrl, and said she 'lowed
Sne'd ruther see her in her shroud,
  I *writ* to Marthy Ellen—

That is, I kindo' tuck my pen
In hand, and stated whur and when
The undersigned would be that night,
With two good hosses saddled right
Fer lively travelin' in case
Her folks 'ud like to jine the race.
She sent the same note back, and writ
"The rose is red!" right under it—
  "Your'n allus, Marthy Ellen."

That's all, I reckon—Nothin' more
To tell but what you've heerd afore—
The same old story, sweeter though
Fer all the trouble, don't you know.
Old-fashioned name! and yit it's jest
As purty as the purtiest,
And more'n that, I'm here to say
I'll live a-thinking thataway,
  And die fer Marthy Elien!

MOON-DROWNED.

'TWAS THE HEIGHT of the fête when we quitted the
        riot,
  And quietly stole to the terrace alone,
Where, pale as the lovers that ever swear by it,
  The moon it gazed down as a god from his throne.
We stood there enchanted.—And O the delight of
  The sight of the stars and the moon and the sea,
And the infinite skies of that opulent night of
  Purple and gold and ivory !

The lisp of the lip of the ripple just under—
  The half-awake nightingale's dream in the yews—
Came up from the water, and down from the wonder
  Of shadowy foliage, drowsed with the dews,—
Unsteady the firefly's taper—unsteady
  The poise of the stars, and their light in the tide,
As it struggled and writhed in caress of the eddy,
  As love in the billowy breast of a bride.

The far-away lilt of the waltz rippled to us,
  And through us the exquisite thrill of the air :
Like the scent of bruised bloom was her breath, and its
        dew was
  Not honier-sweet than her warm kisses were.
We stood there enchanted.—And O the delight of
  The sight of the stars and the moon nad the sea,
And the infinite skies of that opulent night of
  Purple and gold and ivory !

LONG AFORE HE KNOWED WHO SANTY-CLAUS WUZ.

JES' A LITTLE bit o' feller—I remember still,—
    Ust to almost *cry* fer Christmas, like a youngster
      will.
Fourth o' July 's nothin' to it !—New-Year's ai n't a smell :
Easter-Sunday—Circus-day—jes' all dead in the shell !
Lordy, though! at night, you know, to set around and hear
The old folks work the story off about the sledge and deer,
And " Santy " skootin' round the roof, all wrapped in fur
      and fuzz—
Long afore
          I knowed who
                    " Santy-Claus " wuz !

Ust to wait, and set up late, a week er two ahead :
Could n't hardly keep awake, ner would n't go to bed :
Kittle stewin' on the fire, and Mother settin' here
Darnin' socks, and rockin' in the skreeky rockin'-cheer ;
Pap gap', and wunder where it wuz the money went,
And quar'l with his frosted heels, and spill his liniment:
And me a-dreamin' sleigh-bells when the clock 'ud whir
      and buzz,
Long afore
          I knowed who
                    " Santy-Claus " wuz !

Size the fire-place up, and figger how " Old Santy " could
Manage to come down the chimbly, like they said he would:
Wisht that I could hide and see him—wundered what
      he 'd say
Ef he ketched a feller layin' fer him thataway !

But I *bet* on him, and *liked* him, same as ef he had
Turned to pat me on the back and say, " Look here, my lad,
Here 's my pack,—jes' he'p yourse'f, like all good boys
    does !"
Long afore
        I knowed who
              " Santy-Claus " wuz !

Wisht that yarn was *true* about him, as it 'peared to be—
Truth made out o' lies like that-un 's good enough fer me!—
Wisht I still wuz so confidin' I could jes' go wild
Over hangin' up my stockin's, like the little child
Climbin' in my lap to-night, and beggin' me to tell
'Bout them reindeers, and " Old Santy " that she loves so
    well
I 'm half sorry fer this little-girl-sweetheart of his—
Long afore
        She knows who
              " Santy-Claus " is !

DEAR HANDS.

THE TOUCHES of her hands are like the fall
  Of velvet snowflakes; like the touch of down
The peach just brushes 'gainst the garden wall;
The flossy fondlings of the thistle-wisp
    Caught in the crinkle of a leaf of brown
The blighting frost hath turned from green to crisp.

Soft as the falling of the dusk at night,
The touches of her hands, and the delight—
    The touches of her hands !
The touches of her hands are like the dew
That falls so softly down no one e'er knew
The touch thereof save lovers like to one
Astray in lights where ranged Endymion.

O rarely soft, the touches of her hands,
As drowsy zephyrs in enchanted lands ;
    Or pulse of dying fay ; or fairy sighs ;
Or—in between the midnight and the dawn,
When long unrest and tears and fears are gone—
    Sleep, smoothing down the lids of weary eyes.

THIS MAN JONES.

THIS MAN JONES was what you'd call
A feller 'at had no sand at all ;
Kind o' consumpted, and undersize,
And sallor-complected, with big sad eyes,
And a kind-of-a sort-of-a hang-dog style,
And a sneakin' sort-of-a half-way smile
'At kind o' give him away to us
As a preacher, maybe, er somepin' wuss.

Did n't take with the gang—well, no—
But still we managed to use him, though,—
Coddin' the gilly along the rout',
And drivin' the stakes 'at he pulled out—
Fer I was one of the bosses then,
And of course stood in with the canvasmen ;
And the way we put up jobs, you know,
On this man Jones jes' beat the show !

Ust to rattle him scandalous,
And keep the feller a-dodgin' us.
And a-shyin' round half skeered to death,
And afeerd to whimper above his breath ;
Give him a cussin', and then a kick,
And then a kind-of-a back-hand lick—
Jes' fer the fun of seein' him climb
Around with a head on most the time.

But what was the curioust thing to me,
Was along o' the party—let me see,—
Who was our "Lion Queen" last year ?—
Mamzelle Zanty, or De La Pierre ?—
Well, no matter—a stunnin' mash,
With a red-ripe lip, and a long eye-lash,
And a figger sich as the angels owns—
And one too many fer this man Jones.

He 'd allus wake in the afternoon,
As the band waltzed in on the lion-tune,
And there, from the time 'at she 'd go in
Till she 'd back out of the cage agin,
He 'd stand, shaky and limber-kneed—
'Specially when she come to " feed
The beasts raw meat with her naked hand "—
And all that business, you understand.

And it *was* resky in that den—
Fer I think she juggled three cubs then,
And a big " green " lion 'at used to smash
Collar-bones fer old Frank Nash ;
And I reckon now she hain 't fergot
The afternoon old " Nero " sot
His paws on *her!*—but as fer me,
It 's a sort-of-a mixed-up mystery:—

Kind o' remember an awful roar,
And see her back fer the bolted door—
See the cage rock—heerd her call
" God have mercy!" and that was all—
Fer they ain 't no livin' man can tell
What it 's like when a thousand yell
In female tones, and a thousand more
Howl in bass till their throats is sore!

But the keeper said 'at dragged her out,
They heerd some feller laugh and shout—
" Save her ! Quick ! I 've got the cuss !"
And yit she waked and smiled on *us!*
And we dare n't flinch, fer the doctor said,
Seein' as this man Jones was dead,
Better to jes' not let her know
Nothin' o' that fer a week er so.

TO MY GOOD MASTER.

IN FANCY, always, at thy desk, thrown wide,
   Thy most betreasured books ranged neighborly—
   The rarest rhymes of every land and sea
And curious tongue—thine old face glorified,—
Thou haltest thy glib quill, and, laughing-eyed,
   Givest hale welcome even unto me,
   Profaning thus thine attic's sanctity,
To briefly visit, yet to still abide
Enthralled there of thy sorcery of wit,
   And thy songs' most exceeding dear conceits.
   O lips, cleft to the ripe core of all sweets,
   With poems, like nectar, issuing therefrom,
   Thy gentle utterances do overcome
My listening heart and all the love of it!

WHEN THE GREEN GITS BACK IN THE TREES.

IN SPRING, when the green gits back in the trees,
  And the sun comes out and stays,
And yer boots pulls on with a good tight squeeze,
  And you think of yer barefoot days;
When you ort to work and you want to not,
  And you and yer wife agrees
It's time to spade up the garden lot,
    When the green gits back in the trees—
      Well! work is the least o' *my* idees
      When the green, you know, gits back in the trees!

When the green gits back in the trees, and bees
  Is a-buzzin' aroun' agin,
In that kind of a lazy go-as-you-please
  Old gait they bum roun' in;
When the groun's all bald where the hay-rick stood,
  And the crick's riz, and the breeze
Coaxes the bloom in the old dogwood,
    And the green gits back in the trees,—
      I like, as I say, in sich scenes as these,
      The time when the green gits back in the trees!

When the whole tail-feathers o' wintertime
  Is all pulled out and gone!
And the sap it thaws and begins to climb,
  And the sweat it starts out on
A feller's forred, a-gittin' down
  At the old spring on his knees—
I kind o' like jes' a-loaferin' roun'
    When the green gits back in the trees—
      Jes' a-potterin' roun' as I—durn—please—
      When the green, you know, gits back in the trees!

AT BROAD RIPPLE.

AH, LUXURY! Beyond the heat
And dust of town, with dangling feet,
Astride the rock below the dam,
In the cool shadows where the calm
Rests on the stream again, and all
Is silent save the waterfall,—
I bait my hook and cast my line,
And feel the best of life is mine.

No high ambition may I claim—
I angle not for lordly game
Of trout, or bass, or wary bream—
A black perch reaches the extreme
Of my desires ; and "goggle-eyes "
Are not a thing that I despise ;
A sunfish, or a "chub," or "cat "—
A "silver-side "—yea, even that !

In eloquent tranquility
The waters lisp and talk to me.
Sometimes, far out, the surface breaks,
As some proud bass an instant shakes
His glittering armor in the sun,
And romping ripples, one by one,
Come dallying across the space
Where undulates my smiling face.

The river's story flowing by,
Forever sweet to ear and eye,
Forever tenderly begun—
Forever new and never done.
Thus lulled and sheltered in a shade
Where never feverish cares invade,
I bait my hook and cast my line,
And feel the best of life is mine.

WHEN OLD JACK DIED.

I.

WHEN old Jack died, we staid from school (they said,
At home, we need n't go that day), and none
Of us ate any breakfast—only one,
And that was Papa—and his eyes were red
When he came round where we were, by the shed
Where Jack was lying, half way in the sun
And half way in the shade.   When we begun
To cry out loud, Pa turned and dropped his head
And went away; and Mamma, she went back
Into the kitchen.   Then, for a long while,
All to ourselves, like, we stood there and cried.
We thought so many good things of Old Jack.
And funny things—although we did n't smile—
We could n't only cry when Old Jack died.

II.

When Old Jack died, it seemed a human friend
Had suddenly gone from us; that some face
That we had loved to fondle and embrace
From babyhood, no more would condescend
To smile on us forever.   We might bend
With tearful eyes above him, interlace
Our chubby fingers o'er him, romp and race,
Plead with him, call and coax—aye, we might send
The old halloo up for him, whistle, hist,
(If sobs had let us) or, as wildly vain,
Snapped thumbs, called "speak," and he had not replied:
We might have gone down on our knees and kissed
The tousled ears, and yet they must remain
Deaf, motionless, we knew—when Old Jack died.

III.

When Old Jack died, it seemed to us, some way,
That all the other dogs in town were pained
With our bereavement, and some that were chained,
Even, unslipped their collars on that day
To visit Jack in state, as though to pay
A last, sad tribute there, while neighbors craned
Their heads above the high board fence, and deigned
To sigh " Poor dog!" remembering how they
Had cuffed him, when alive, perchance, because,
For love of them he leaped to lick their hands—
Now, that he could not, were they satisfied ?
We children thought that, as we crossed his paws,
And o'er his grave, 'way down the bottom-lands,
Wrote " Our First Love Lies Here," when Old Jack died.

DOC SIFERS.

OF ALL THE DOCTORS I could cite you to in
    this-'ere town
Doc Sifers is my favorite, jes' take him up and down!
Count in the Bethel Neighberhood, and Rollins, and Big
    Bear,
And Sifers' standin's jes' as good as ary doctor's there!

There's old Doc Wick, and Glenn, and Hall, and Wurg-
    ler, and McVeigh,
But I'll buck Sifers 'ginst 'em all and down 'em any day!
Most old Wick ever knowed, I s'pose, was *whisky!*
    Wurgler—well,
He et morphine—ef actions shows, and facts' reliable!

But Sifers—though he ain't no sot. he's got his faults;
    and yit
When you *git* Sifers onc't, you've got *a doctor*, don't
    fergit!
He ain't much at his office. er his house, er anywhere
You'd natchurly think certain fer to ketch the feller there.—

But don't blame Doc: he's got all sorts o' cur'ous no-
    tions—as
The feller says, his odd-come-shorts, like smart men
    mostly has.
He'll more 'n like be potter 'n 'round the Blacksmith Shop;
    er in
Some back lot, spadin' up the ground, er gradin' it agin.

Er at the workbench, planin' things; er buildin' little
    traps
To ketch birds; galvenizin' rings; er graftin' plums, per-
    haps.
Make anything! good as the best!—a gunstock—er a flute;
He whittled out a set o' chesstmen onc't o' laurel root.

Durin' the Army—got his trade o' surgeon there—I own
To-day a finger-ring Doc made out of a Sesesh bone!
An' glued a fiddle onc't fer me—jes' all so busted you
'D a throwed the thing away, but he fixed her as good
     as new!

And take Doc, now, in *ager*, say, er *biles*, er *rheumatiz*,
And all afflictions thataway, and he's the best they is!
Er janders—milksick—I do n't keer—k-yore anything he
     tries—
A abscess; getherin' in yer yeer; er granilated eyes!

There was the Widder Daubenspeck they all give up fer
     dead;
A blame cowbuncle on her neck, and clean out of her
     head!
First had this doctor, what's-his-name, from "Puddles-
     burg," and then
This littie red-head, "Burnin' Shame" they call him—Dr.
     Glenn.

And they "consulted" on the case, and claimed she'd haf
     to die,—
I jes' was joggin' by the place, and heerd her dorter cry,
And stops and calls her to the fence; and I-says-I, "Let
     me
Send Sifers—bet you fifteen cents he'll k-yore her!"
     "Well," says she,

"Light out!" she says: And, lipp-tee-cut! I loped in town,
     and rid
'Bout two hours more to find him, but I kussed him when
     I did!
He was down at the Gunsmith Shop a-stuffin' birds! Says
     he,
"My sulky's broke." Says I, "You hop right on and
     ride with me!"

ĭ got him there.—" Well, Aunty, ten days k-yores you,"
    Sifers said,
'But what 's yer idy livin' when yer jes' as good as dead?"
And there 's Dave Banks—jes' back from war without a
    scratch—one day
Got ketched up in a sickle-bar, a reaper runaway.—

His shoulders, arms, and hands and legs jes' sawed in
    strips! And Jake
Dunn starts fer Sifers—feller begs to shoot him fer God-
    sake.
Doc, 'course, was gone, but he had penned the notice, "At
    Big Bear—
Be back to-morry; Gone to 'tend the Bee Convention
    there."

But Jake, he tracked him—rid and rode the whole en-
    durin' night!
And 'bout the time the roosters crowed they both hove
    into sight.
Doc had to ampitate, but 'greed to save Dave's arms, and
    swore
He could a-saved his legs ef he 'd ben there the day before.

Like when his wife's own mother died 'fore Sifers could
    be found,
And all the neighbers fer and wide a' all jes' chasin' round;
Tel finally—I had to laugh—it 's jes' like Doc, you know,—
Was learnin' fer to telegraph, down at the old deepo.

But all they 're faultin' Sifers fer, there 's none of 'em kin
    say
He 's biggoty, er keerless, er not posted anyway;
He ain't built on the common plan of doctors now-a-days,
He 's jes' a great, big, brainy man—that 's where the
    trouble lays!

AT NOON—AND MIDNIGHT.

FAR IN THE NIGHT, and yet no rest for him! The
    pillow next his own
The wife's sweet face in slumber pressed—yet he awake—
    alone! alone!
In vain he courted sleep;—one thought would ever in his
    heart arise,—
The harsh words that at noon had brought the teardrops
    to her eyes.

Slowly on lifted arm he raised and listened.   All was still
    as death;
He touched her forehead as he gazed, and listened yet,
    with bated breath:
Still silently, as though he prayed, his lips moved lightly
    as she slept—
For God was with him, and he laid his face with hers **and**
    wept.

12

A Wild Irishman

A WILD IRISHMAN.

NOT very many years ago the writer was for some months stationed at South Bend, a thriving little city of northern Indiana, its main population on the one side of the St. Joseph river, but quite a respectable fraction thereof taking its industrial way to the opposite shore, and there gaining an audience and a hearing in the rather imposing growth and hurly-burly of its big manufactories, and the consequent rapid appearance of multitudinous neat cottages, tenement houses and business blocks. A stranger, entering South Bend proper on any ordinary day, will be at some loss to account for its prosperous appearance—its flagged and bowldered streets —its handsome mercantile blocks, banks, and business houses generally. Reasoning from cause to effect, and seeing but a meager sprinkling of people on the streets throughout the day, and these seeming, for the most part, merely idlers, and in no wise accessory to the evident thrift and opulence of their surroundings, the observant stranger will be puzzled at the situation. But when evening comes, and the outlying foundries, sewing-machine,

wagon, plow, and other "works," together
with the paper-mills and all the nameless in-
dustries—when the operations of all these are
suspended for the day, and the workmen and
workwomen loosed from labor—then, as this
vast army suddenly invades and overflows
bridge, roadway, street and lane, the startled
stranger will fully comprehend the why and
wherefore of the city's high prosperity. And,
once acquainted with the people there, the
fortunate sojourner will find no ordinary culture and intelligence, and, as certainly, he will
meet with a social spirit and a wholesouled
heartiness that will make the place a lasting
memory. The town, too, is the home of many
world-known notables, and a host of local
celebrities, the chief of which latter class I
found, during my stay there, in the person of
Tommy Stafford, or "The Wild Irishman" as
everybody called him.

"Talk of odd fellows and eccentric characters," said Major Blowney, my employer, one
afternoon, "you must see our 'Wild Irishman' here before you say you've yet found
the queerest, brightest, cleverest chap in all
your travels. What d'ye say, Stockford?"
And the Major paused in his work of charging
cartridges for his new breech-loading shotgun
and turned to await his partner's response.

Stockford, thus addressed, paused above the shield-sign he was lettering, slowly smiling as be dipped and trailed his pencil through the ivory black upon a bit of broken glass and said, in his deliberate, half-absent-minded way,—"Is it Tommy you're telling him about?" and then, with a gradual broadening of the smile, he went on, "Well, I should say so. Tommy! What's come of the fellow, anyway? I haven't seen him since his last bout with the mayor, on his trial for shakin' up that fast-horse man."

"The fast-horse man got just exactly what he needed, too," said the genial Major, laughing, and mopping his perspiring brow. "The fellow was barkin' up the wrong stump when he tackled Tommy! Got beat in the trade, at his own game, you know, and wound up by an insult that no Irishman would take; and Tommy just naturally wore out the hall carpet of the old hotel with him!"

"And then collared and led him to the mayor's office himself, they say!"

"Oh, he did!" said the Major, with a dash of pride in the confirmation; "that's Tommy all over!"

"Funny trial, was n't it?" continued the ruminating Stockford.

"Was n't it though?" laughed the Major.

"The porter's testimony: You see, he was for Tommy, of course, and on examination testified that the horse-man struck Tommy first. And there Tommy broke in with: "He's a-meanin' well, yer Honor, but he's lyin' to ye—he's lyin' to ye. No livin' man iver struck me first—nor last, nayther, for the matter o' that!' And I thought—the—court —would—die!" concluded the Major, in a like imminent state of merriment.

"Yes, and he said if he struck him first," supplemented Stockford, "he'd like to know why the horseman was 'wearin' all the black eyes, and the blood, and the boomps on the head of um!' And it's that talk of his that got him off with so light a fine!"

"As it always does," said the Major, coming to himself abruptly and looking at his watch. "Stock', you say you're not going along with our duck-shooting party this time? The old Kankakee is just lousy with 'em this season!"

"Can't go possibly," said Stockford, "not on account of the work at all, but the folks at home ain't just as well as I'd like to see them, and I'll stay here till they're better. Next time I'll try and be ready for you. Going to take Tommy, of course?"

"Of course! Got to have 'The Wild Irish-

man' with us!   I 'm going around to find him
now."   Then turning to me the Major continued, " Suppose you get on your coat and
hat and come along?   It 's the best chance
you 'll ever have to meet Tommy.   It 's late
anyhow, and Stockford 'll get along without
you.   Come on."

" Certainly," said Stockford; " go ahead.
And you can take him ducking, too, if he
wants to go."

" But he does n't want to go—and wo n't
go," replied the Major with a commiserative
glance at me.   " Says he does n't know a
duck from a poll-parrot—nor how to load a
shotgun—and could n't hit a house if he were
inside of it and the door shut.   Admits that
he nearly killed his uncle once, on the other
side of a tree, with a squirrel runnin' down it.
Do n't want him along! "

Reaching the street with the genial Major,
he gave me this advice: " Now, when you
meet Tommy, you must n't take all he says
for dead earnest, and you must n't believe, because he talks loud, and in italics every other
word, that he wants to do all the talking and
wo n't be interfered with.   That 's the way he 's
apt to strike folks at first—but it 's their mistake, not his.   Talk back to him—controvert
him whenever he 's aggressive in the utter-

ance of his opinions, and if you 're only honest in the announcement of your own ideas and beliefs, he 'll like you all the better for standing by them. He 's quick-tempered, and perhaps a trifle sensitive, so share your greater patience with him, and he 'll pay you back by fighting for you at the drop of the hat. In short, he 's as nearly typical of his gallant country's brave, impetuous, fun-loving individuality as such a likeness can exist."

"But is he quarrelsome?" I asked.

"Not at all. There 's the trouble. If he 'd only quarrel there 'd be no harm done. Quarreling 's cheap, and Tommy 's extravagant. A big blacksmith here, the other day, kicked some boy out of his shop, and Tommy, on his cart, happened to be passing at the time ; and he just jumped off without a word, and went in and worked on that fellow for about three minutes, with such disastrous results that they could n't tell his shop from a slaughter-house ; paid an assault and battery fine, and gave the boy a dollar beside, and the whole thing was a positive luxury to him. But I guess we 'd better drop the subject, for here 's his cart, and here 's Tommy. Hi! there, you 'Fardown' Irish Mick!" called the Major, in affected antipathy, "been out raiding the honest farmers' hen-roosts again, have you?"

We had halted at a corner grocery and produce store, as I took it, and the smooth-faced,
shave-headed man in woolen shirt, short vest,
and suspenderless trousers so boisterously addressed by the Major, was just lifting from the
back of his cart a coop of cackling chickens.

"Arrah! ye blasted Kerryonian!" replied
the handsome fellow, depositing the coop on
the curb and straightening his tall, slender
figure; " I were jist thinking of yez and the
ducks, and here ye come quackin' into the
prisence of r'yalty, wid yer canvas-back suit
upon ye and the shwim-skins bechuxt yer
toes! How air yez, anyhow—and air we startin' for the Kankakee by the nixt post?"

" We 're to start just as soon as we get the
boys together," said the Major, shaking hands.
"The crowd's to be at Andrews' by 4, and it's
fully that now; so come on at once. We'll
go 'round by Munson's and have Hi send a
boy to look after your horse. Come; and I
want to introduce my friend here to you, and
we'll all want to smoke and jabber a little in
appropriate seclusion. Come on." And the
impatient Major had linked arms with his hes-
itating ally and myself, and was turning the
corner of the street.

" It's an hour's work I have yet wid the
squawkers," mildly protested Tommy, still

hanging back and stepping a trifle high; "but, as one Irishman would say til another, 'Ye 're wrong, but I 'm wid ye!'"

And five minutes later the three of us had joined a very jolly party in a snug back room, with

> "The chamber walls depicted all around
>   With portraitures of huntsman, hawk, and hound,
>   And the hurt deer;"

and where, as well, drifted over the olfactory intelligence a certain subtle, warm-breathed aroma, that genially combatted the chill and darkness of the day without, and, resurrecting long-dead Christmases, brimmed the grateful memory with all comfortable cheer.

A dozen hearty voices greeted the appearance of Tommy and the Major, the latter adroitly pushing the jovial Irishman to the front, with a mock-heroic introduction to the general company, at the conclusion of which Tommy, with his hat tucked under the left elbow, stood bowing with a grace of pose and presence Lord Chesterfield might have applauded.

"Gintlemen," said Tommy, settling back upon his heels and admiringly contemplating the group; "Gintlemen, I congratu-late yez wid a pride that shoves the thumbs o' me into the arrum-holes of me weshkit! At the inshtigation of the bowld *O*'Blowney—axin' the gintleman's pardon—I am here wid no silver tongue of illoquence to para-lyze yez, but I am prisent, as has been ripresinted, to jine wid yez in a stupendeous waste of gun-powder, and duck-shot, and 'high-wines,' and ham sand-witches, upon the silvonian banks of the ragin' Kankakee, where the 'di-dipper' tips ye good-bye wid his tail, and the wild loon skoots like a sky-rocket for his exiled home in the alien dunes of the wild morass— or, as Tommy Moore so illegantly describes the blashted birrud,—

> 'Away to the dizhmal shwamp he shpeeds—
>   His path is rugged and sore,
> Through tangled juniper, beds of reeds,
> And many a fen where the serpent feeds,
>   *And birrud niver flew before—*
>   *And niver will fly any more*

if iver he arrives back safe into civilization again—and I've been in the poultry business long enough to know the private opinion and personal integrity of ivery fowl that flies the air or roosts on poles. But, changin' the subject of my few small remarks here, and thankin yez wid an overflowin' heart but a dhry tongue, I have the honor to propose, gintlemen, long life and health to ivery mother's son o' yez, and success to the 'Duck-hunters of Kankakee.'"

"The duck-hunters of the Kankakee!" chorussed the elated party in such musical uproar that for a full minute the voice of the enthusiastic Major—who was trying to say something—could not be heard. Then he said:

"I want to propose that theme—'The Duck-hunters of the Kankakee', for one of Tommy's improvizations. I move we have a song now from Tommy on the 'Duck-hunters of the Kankakee.'"

"Hurra! Hurra! A song from Tommy," cried the crowd. "Make us up a song, and put us all into it! A song from Tommy! A song! A song!"

There was a queer light in the eye of the Irishman. I observed him narrowly—expectantly. Often I had read of this phenomenal art of improvised ballad-singing, but had always remained a little skeptical in regard to the possibility of such a feat. Even in the notable instances of this gift as displayed by the very clever Theodore Hook, I had always half suspected some prior preparation—some adroit forecasting of the sequence that seemed the instant inspiration of his witty verses.

Here was evidently to be a test example, and
I was all alert to mark its minutest detail.

The clamor had subsided, and Tommy had
drawn a chair near to and directly fronting the
Major's. His right hand was extended,
closely grasping the right hand of his friend
which he scarce perceptibly, though measur-
edly, lifted and let fall throughout the length
of all the curious performance. The voice
was not unmusical, nor was the quaint old
ballad-air adopted by the singer unlovely in
the least; simply a monotony was evident
that accorded with the levity and chance-fin-
ish of the improvisation—and that the song
was improvised on the instant I am certain—
though in no wise remarkable, for other reasons, in rhythmic worth or finish. And while
his smiling auditors all drew nearer, and leant,
with parted lips to catch every syllable, the
words of the strange melody trailed unhesitat-
ingly into the lines literally as here subjoined :

> " One gloomy day in the airly Fall,
>   Whin the sunshine had no chance at all—
>   No chance at all for to gleam and shine
>   And lighten up this heart of mine:

> " 'Twas in South Bend, that famous town,
>   Whilst I were a-strollin' round and round,
>   I met some friends and they says to me:
> ' It 's a hunt we 'll take on the Kankakee!' "

"Hurra for the Kankakee! Give it to us, Tommy!' cried an enthused voice between verses. "Now give it to the Major!" And the song went on:—

> "There's Major Blowney leads the van,
>   As crack a shot as an Irishman,—
>   For its the duck is a tin decoy
>   That his owld shotgun can't destroy:

And a half a dozen jubilant palms patted the Major's shoulders, and his ruddy, good-natured face beamed with delight. "Now give it to the rest of 'em, Tommy!" chuckled the Major. And the song continued:—

> "And along wid 'Hank' is Mick Maharr,
>   And Barney Pince, at 'The Shamrock' bar—
>   There's Barney Pinch, wid his heart so true;
>   And the Andrews Brothers they'll go too."

"Hold on, Tommy!" chipped in one of the Andrews; "you must give 'the Andrews Brothers' a better advertisement than that! Turn us on a full verse, can't you?"

"Make 'em pay for it if you do!" said the Major, in an undertone. And Tommy promptly amended:—

> "O, the Andrews Brothers, they'll be there,
>   Wid good se-gyars and wine to shpare,—
>   They'll treat us here on fine champagne,
>   And whin we're there they'll treat us again."

The applause here was vociferous, and only discontinued when a box of Havanas stood open on the table. During the momentary lull thus occasioned, I caught the Major's twinkling eyes glancing evasively toward me, as he leant whispering some further instructions to Tommy, who again took up his desultory ballad, while I turned and fled for the street, catching, however, as I went, and high above the laughter of the crowd, the satire of this quatrain to its latest line —

> " But R-R-Riley he 'll not go, I guess,
> Lest he 'd get lost in the wil-der-ness,
> And so in the city he will shtop
> For to curl his hair in the barber shop."

It was after six when I reached the hotel, but I had my hair trimmed before I went in to supper. The style of trimming adopted then I still rigidly adhere to, and call it " the Tommy Stafford stubble-crop."

Ten days passed before I again saw the Major. Immediately upon his return—it was late afternoon when I heard of it—I determined to take my evening walk out the long street toward his pleasant home and call upon him there This I did, and found him in a wholesome state of fatigue, slippers and easy chair, enjoying his pipe on the piazza. Of

course, he was overflowing with happy rem-
iniscences of the hunt—the wood-and-water-
craft—boats—ambushes—decoys, and tramp,
and camp, and so on, without end;—but I
wanted to hear him talk of "The Wild Irishman"—Tommy; and I think, too, now, that
the sagacious Major secretly read my desires
all the time. To be utterly frank with the
reader I will admit that I not only think the
Major divined my interest in Tommy, but I
know he did; for at last, as though reading
my very thoughts, he abruptly said, after a
long pause, in which he knocked the ashes
from his pipe and refilled and lighted it:—
"Well, all I know of ' The Wild Irishman ' I
can tell you in a very few words—that is, if
you care at all to listen?" And the crafty old
Major seemed to hesitate.

"Go on—go on!" I said, eagerly.

"About forty years ago," resumed the Major, placidly, "in the little, old, unheard-of
town Karnteel, County Tyrone, Province Ul-
ster, Ireland, Tommy Stafford—in spite of the
contrary opinion of his wretchedly poor parents—was fortunate enough to be born. And
here, again, as I advised you the other day,
you must be prepared for constant surprises in
the study of Tommy's character."

"Go on," I said; "I'm prepared for anything."

The Major smiled profoundly and continued :—

"Fifteen years ago, when he came to Amer-
ica—and the Lord only knows how he got
the passage-money—he brought his widowed
mother with him here, and has supported, and
is still supporting her.   Besides," went on the
still secretly smiling Major, "the fellow has
actually found time, through all his adversi-
ties, to pick up quite a smattering of education,
here and there—"

"Poor fellow!" I broke in, sympathizingly,
"what a pity it is that he could n't have had
such advantages earlier in life," and as I re-
called the broad brogue of the fellow, together
with his careless dress, recognizing beneath
it all the native talent and brilliancy of a mind
of most uncommon worth, I could not restrain
a deep sigh of compassion and regret.

The Major was leaning forward in the gath-
ering dusk, and evidently studying my own
face, the expression of which, at that moment,
was very grave and solemn, I am sure.   He
suddenly threw himself backward in his chair,
in an uncontrollable burst of laughter.   "Oh,
I just can't keep it up any longer," he exclaimed.

"Keep what up?" I queried, in a perfect maze of bewilderment and surprise. "Keep what up?" I repeated.

"Why, all this twaddle, farce, travesty and by-play regarding Tommy! You know I warned you, over and over, and you must n't blame me for the deception. I never thought you'd take it so in earnest!" and here the jovial Major again went into convulsions of laughter.

"But I don't understand a word of it all," I cried, half frenzied with the gnarl and tangle of the whole affair. "What 'twaddle, farce and by-play,' is it anyhow?" And in my vexation, I found myself on my feet and striding nervously up and down the paved walk that joined the street with the piazza, pausing at last and confronting the Major almost petulantly. "Please explain," I said, controlling my vexation with an effort.

The Major arose. "Your striding up and down there reminds me that a little stroll on the street might do us both good," he said. "Will you wait until I get a coat and hat?"

He rejoined me a moment later, and we passed through the open gate; and saying, "Let's go down this way," he took my arm and turned into a street, where, cooling as the dusk was, the thick maples lining the walk, seemed to throw a special shade of tranquility upon us.

"What I meant was "—began the Major, in low, serious voice,—"What I meant was—simply this: Our friend Tommy, though the truest Irishman in the world, is a man quite the opposite everyway of the character he has appeared to you. All that rich brogue of his is assumed. Though he's poor, as I told you, when he came here, his native quickness, and his marvelous resources, tact, judgment, business qualities—all have helped him to the equivalent of a liberal education. His love of the humorous and the ridiculous is unbounded ; but he has serious moments, as well, and at such times is as dignified and refined in speech and manner as any man you'd find in a thousand. He is a good speaker, can stir a political convention to fomentation when he gets fired up; and can write an article for the press that goes spang to the spot. He gets into a great many personal encounters of a rather undignified character ; but they are almost invariably bred of his innate interest in the 'under dog,' and the fire and tow of his impetuous nature."

My companion had paused here, and was looking through some printed slips in his pocket-book. "I wanted you to see some of

the fellow's articles in print, but I have nothing of importance here—only some of his
'doggerel,' as he calls it, and you 've had a
sample of that. But here 's a bit of the upper
spirit of the man—and still another that you
should hear him recite. You can keep them
both if you care to. The boys all fell in love
with that last one, particularly, hearing his
rendition of it. So we had a lot printed, and
I have two or three left. Put these two in your
pocket and read at your leisure."

But I read them there and then, as eagerly,
too, as I append them here and now. The first
is called—

SAYS HE.

" Whatever the weather may be," says he—
 " Whatever the weather may be,
It 's plaze, if ye will, an' I 'll say me say,—
Supposin' to-day was the winterest day,
Wud the weather be changing because ye cried,
Or the snow be grass were ye crucified?
The best is to make your own summer," says he,
" Whatever the weather may be," says he—
 " Whatever the weather may be!

" Whatever the weather may be," says he—
 " Whatever the weather may be,
It 's the songs ye sing, an' the smiles ye wear,
That 's a-makin' the sunshine everywhere;
An' the world of gloom is a world of glee,
Wid the bird in the bush, an' the bud in the tree,
An' the fruit on the stim of the bough," says he,
" Whatever the weather may be," says he—
 " Whatever the weather may be!

"Whatever the weather may be," says he—
"Whatever the weather may be,
Ye can bring the Spring, wid its green an' gold,
An' the grass in the grove where the snow lies cold,
An' ye 'll warm yer back, wid a smiling face,
As ye sit at yer heart like an owld fire-place,
An' toast the toes o' yer soul," says he,
"Whatever the weather may be," says he—
"Whatever the weather may be!"

"Now," said the Major, peering eagerly above my shoulder, "go on with the next. To my liking, it is even better than the first. A type of character you 'll recognize.—The same 'broth of a boy,' only *Americanized*, don 't you know."

And I read the scrap entitled—

CHAIRLEY BURKE.

It 's Chairley Burke 's in town, b'ys! He 's down til
"Jamesy's Place,"
Wid a bran' new shave upon 'um, an' the fhwhuskers aff
his face;
He 's quit the Section Gang last night, and yez can chalk
it down,
There 's goin' to be the divil's toime, sence Chairley
Burke 's in town.

It 's treatin' iv'ry b'y he is, an' poundin' on the bar
Till iv'ry man he 's drinkin' wid must shmoke a foine
cigar;
An' Missus Murphy's little Kate, that 's comin' there for
beer,
Can't pay wan cint the bucketful, the whilst that Chairley 's here!

He's joompin' oor the tops o' sthools, the both forninst
    an' back!
He'll lave yez pick the blessed flure, an' walk the straight-
    est crack!
He's liftin' barrels wid his teeth, and singin' "Garry
    Owen,"
Till all the house be strikin' hands, sence Chairley Burke's
    in town.

The Road-Yaird hands comes dhroppin' in, an' niver goin'
    back;
An' there's two freights upon the switch—the wan on
    aither track—
An' Mr. Gearry, from The Shops, he's mad enough to
    swear,
An' durst n't spake a word but grin, the whilst that
    Chairley's there!

Oh! Chairley! Chairley! Chairley Burke! ye divil, wid
    yer ways
O' dhrivin' all the throubles aff, these dark an' gloomy
    days!
Ohone! that it's meself, wid all the griefs I have to drown,
Must lave me pick to resht a bit, sence Chairley Burke's
    in town!

"Before we turn back, now," said the smiling Major, as I stood lingering over the indefinable humor of the last refrain, "before
we turn back I want to show you something
eminently characteristic. Come this way a
half dozen steps."

As he spoke I looked up, to first observe
that we had paused before a handsome square
brick residence, centering a beautiful smooth

.awn, its emerald only littered with the light gold of the earliest autumn leaves. On either side of the trim walk that led up from the gate to the carved stone ballusters of the broad piazza, with its empty easy chairs, were graceful vases, frothing over with late blossoms, and wreathed with laurel-looking vines ; and, luxuriantly lacing the border of the pave that turned the further corner of the house, blue, white and crimson, pink and violet, went fading in perspective as my gaze followed the gesture of the Major's.

" Here, come a little further. Now do you see that man there? "

Yes, I could make out a figure in the deepening dusk—the figure of a man on the back stoop—a tired looking man, in his shirt-sleeves, who sat upon a low chair—no, not a chair—an empty box. He was leaning forward with his elbows on his knees, and the hands dropped limp. He was smoking, too, I could barely see his pipe, and but for the odor of very strong tobacco, would not have known he had a pipe. Why does the master of the house permit his servants to so desecrate this beautiful home? I thought.

" Well, shall we go now? " said the Major.

I turned silently and we retraced our steps.

I think neither of us spoke for the distance of a square.

"Guess you did n't know the man there on the back porch?" said the Major.

"No; why?" I asked dubiously.

"I hardly thought you would, and besides the poor fellow 's tired, and it was best not to disturb him," said the Major.

"Why; who was it—some one I know?"

"It was Tommy."

"Oh," said I, inquiringly, "he 's employed there in some capacity?"

"Yes, as master of the house."

"You don 't mean it?"

"I certainly do. He owns it, and made every cent of the money that paid for it!" said the Major proudly. "That 's why I wanted you particularly to note that 'eminent characteristic' I spoke of. Tommy could just as well be sitting, with a fine cigar, on the front piazza in an easy chair, as, with his dhudeen, on the back porch, on an empty box, where every night you 'll find him. Its the unconscious dropping back into the old ways of his father, and his father's father, and his father's father's father. In brief, he sits there the poor lorn symbol of the long oppression of his race."

Ragweed and Fennel

WHEN MY DREAMS COME TRUE.

I.

WHEN MY dreams come true—when my dreams
come true—
Shall I lean from out my casement, in the starlight and
the dew,
To listen—smile and listen to the tinkle of the strings
Of the sweet guitar my lover's fingers fondle, as he sings?
And as the nude moon slowly, slowly shoulders into view,
Shall I vanish from his vision—when my dreams come true?

When my dreams come true—shall the simple gown I wear
Be changed to softest satin, and my maiden-braided hair
Be raveled into flossy mists of rarest, fairest gold,
To be m'nted into kisses, more than any heart can hold?—
Or "the summer of my tresses" shall my lover liken to
"The fervor of his passion"—when my dreams come true?

II.

When my dreams come true—I shall bide among the
sheaves
Of happy harvest meadows; and the grasses and the leaves
Shall lift and lean between me and the splendor of the sun,
Till the noon swoons into twilight, and the gleaners' work
is done—
Save that yet an arm shall bind me, even as the reapers do
The meanest sheaf of harvest—when my dreams come true.

When my dreams come true! when my dreams come true!
True love in all simplicity is fresh and pure as dew;—
The blossom in the blackest mold is kindlier to the eye
Than any lily born of pride that looms against the sky:
And so it is I know my heart will gladly welcome you,
My lowliest of lovers, when my dreams come true.

(163)

A DOS'T O' BLUES.

I' GOT NO patience with blues at all!
  And I ust to kindo talk
Aginst 'em, and claim, 'tel along last Fall,
  They was none in the fambly stock;
But a nephew of mine, from Eelinoy,
  That visited us last year,
He kindo convinct me differunt
  While he was a-stayin' here.

Frum ever'-which way that blues is from,
  They 'd tackle him ever' ways;
They 'd come to him in the night, and come
  On Sundays, and rainy days;
They 'd tackle him in corn-plantin' time,
  And in harvest, and airly Fall,
But a dose 't of blues in the wintertime,
  He 'lowed, was the worst of all!

Said all diseases that ever he had—
  The mumps, er the rheumatiz—
Er ever'-other-day-aigger 's bad
  Purt' nigh as anything is!—
Er a cyarbuncle, say, on the back of his neck,
  Er a felon on his thumb,—
But you keep the blues away from him,
  And all o' the rest could come!

And he 'd moan, "They 's nary a leaf below!
  Ner a spear o' grass in sight!
And the whole wood-pile 's clean under snow!
  And the days is dark as night!

You can't go out—ner you can't stay in—
  Lay down—stand up—ner set!"
And a tetch o' regular tyfoid-blues
  Would double him jest clean shet!

I writ his parents a postal-kyard,
  He could stay 'tel Spring-time come:
And Aprile first, as I rickollect,
  Was the day we shipped him home!
Most o' his relatives, sence then,
  Has either give up, er quit,
Er jest died off; but I understand
  He's the same old color yit!

THE BAT.

I.

THOU DREAD, uncanny thing,
With fuzzy breast and leathern wing,
  In mad, zigzagging flight,
Notching the dusk, and buffeting
  The black cheeks of the night,
    With grim delight!

II.

What witch's hand unhasps
  Thy keen claw-cornered wings
  From under the barn roof, and flings
Thee forth, with chattering gasps,
    To scud the air,
And nip the lady-bug, and tear
Her children's hearts out unaware?

III.

The glow-worm's glimmer, and the bright,
Sad pulsings of the fire-fly's light,
  Are banquet lights to thee.
O less than bird, and worse than beast,
Thou Devil's self, or brat, at least,
  Grate not thy teeth at me!

THE WAY IT WUZ.

LAS' JULY—an', I persume
  'Bout as hot
As the ole Gran'-Jury room
  Where they sot!—
Fight 'twixt Mike an' Dock McGriff—
'Pears to me jes' like as if
  I 'd a dremp' the whole blame thing—
   Allus ha'nts me roun' the gizzard
  When they 're nightmares on the wing,
    An' a feller's blood 's jes' friz!
   Seed the row from a to izzard—
  'Cause I wuz a-standin' as clost to 'em
    As me an' you is!

Tell you the way it wuz—
  An' I do n't want to see,
Like *some* fellers does,
  When they 're goern to be
Any kind o' fuss—
On'y makes a rumpus wuss
  Fer to interfere
   When their dander 's riz—
But I wuz a-standin' as clost to 'em
   As me an' you is!

I wuz kind o' strayin'
  Past the blame saloon—
Heerd some fiddler playin'
  That " ole hee-cup tune!"
Sort o' stopped, you know,
Fer a minit er so,
  And wuz jes' about
     (167)

Settin' down, when—*Jeemses whizz!*
  Whole durn winder-sash fell out!
An' there laid Doc McGriff, and Mike
A-straddlin' him, all bloody-like,
  An' both a-gittin' down to biz!—
An' I wuz a-standin' as clost to 'em
    As me an' you is!

ᴵ wuz the on'y man aroun'—
(Durn old-fogy town!
  'Peared more like, to me,
    Sund'y 'an Saturd'y!)
  Dog come 'crost the road
    An' tuck a smell
      An' put right back;
  Mishler driv by 'ith a load
    O' cantalo'pes he could n't sell—
      Too mad, 'y jack!
  To even ast
  What wuz up, as he went past!
Weather most outrageous hot!—
    Fairly hear it sizz
Roun' Dock an' Mike—till Dock he shot,
    An' Mike he slacked that grip o' his
    An' fell, all spraddled out.   Dock riz
  'Bout half up, a-spittin' red,
    An' shuck his head—
An' I wuz a-standin' as clost to 'em
    As me an' you is!

An' Dock he says,
  A-whisperin'-like,—
"It hain't no use
  A-tryin'!—Mike
    He 's jes' ripped my daylights loose!—

Git that blame-don fiddler to
Let up, an' come out here—You
Got some burryin' to do,—
    Mike makes *one*, an' I expects
In ten seconds I 'll make *two* ' "
    And he drapped back, where he **riz,**
'Crost Mike's body, black and blue,
      Like a great big letter X!—
An' I wuz a-standin' as clost to 'em
    As me an' **you is!**

THE DRUM.

O THE DRUM!
There is some
Intonation in thy grum
Monotony of utterance that strikes the spirit dumb,
As we hear
Through the clear
And unclouded atmosphere,
Thy palpitating syllables roll in upon the ear!

There's a part
Of the art
Of thy music-throbbing heart
That thrills a something in us that awakens with a start,
And in rhyme
With the chime
And exactitude of time,
Goes marching on to glory to thy melody sublime.

And the guest
Of the breast
That thy rolling robs of rest
Is a patriotic spirit as a Continental dressed;
And he looms
From the glooms
Of a century of tombs,
And the blood he spilled at Lexington in living beauty
blooms.

And his eyes
Wear the guise
Of a purpose pure and wise,

(170)

As the love of them is lifted to a something in the skies
That is bright
    Red and white,
        With a blur of starry light,
As it laughs in silken ripples to the breezes day and night.

There are deep
    Hushes creep
        O'er the pulses as they leap,
As thy tumult, fainter growing, on the silence falls asleep,
While the prayer
    Rising there
        Wills the sea and earth and air
As a heritage to Freedom's sons and daughters everywhere.

Then, with sound
    As profound
        As the thunderings resound,
Come thy wild reverberations in a throe that shakes the
    ground,
And a cry
    Flung on high,
        Like the flag it flutters by,
Wings rapturously upward till it nestles in the sky.

O the drum!
    There is some
        Intonation in thy grum
Monotony of utterance that strikes the spirit dumb,
As we hear
    Through the clear
        And unclouded atmosphere,
Thy palpitating syllables roll in upon the ear!

TOM JOHNSON 'S QUIT.

A PASSEL o' the boys last night—
    An' me amongst 'em—kindo got
To talkin' Temper'nce left an' right,
    An' workin' up "blue-ribbon," *hot;*
An' while we was a-countin' jes'
    How many hed gone into hit
An' signed the pledge, some feller says,—
        "Tom Johnson 's quit!"

We laughed, of course—'cause Tom, you know,
    He's spiled more whisky, boy an' man,
And seed more trouble, high an' low,
    Than any chap but Tom could stand:
And so, says I "*He's* too nigh dead
    Fer Temper'nce to benefit!"
The feller sighed agin, and said—
        "Tom Johnson 's quit!"

We all *liked* Tom, an' that was why
    We sorto simmered down agin,
And ast the feller ser'ously
    Ef he wa' n't tryin' to draw us in:
He shuck his head—tuck off his hat—
    Helt up his hand an' opened hit,
An' says, says he, "I 'll *swear* to that—
        Tom Johnson 's quit!"

Well, we was stumpt, an' tickled too,—
    Because we knowed ef Tom *hed* signed
Ther wa' n't no man 'at wore the "blue"
    'At was more honester inclined:

An' then and there we kindo riz,—
   The hull dern gang of us 'at bit—
An' th'owed our hats and let 'er whizz,—
     "*Tom Johnson's quit!*"

I 've heerd 'em holler when the balls
   Was buzzin' 'round us wus 'n bees,
An' when the ole flag on the walls
   Was flappin' o'er the enemy's,
I 've heerd a-many a wild "hooray"
   'At made my heart git up an' git—
But Lord!—to hear 'em shout that way!—
     "*Tom Johnson's quit!*"

But when we saw the chap 'at fetched
   The news wa' n't jinin' in the cheer,
But stood there solemn-like, an' reched
   An' kindo wiped away a tear,
We someway sorto' stilled agin,
   And listened—I kin hear him yit,
His voice a-wobblin' with his chin,—
     " Tom Johnson 's quit—

"I hain't a-givin' you no game—
   I wisht I was! . . . . An hour ago,
This operator—what 's his name—
   The one 'at works at night, you know?—
Went out to flag that Ten Express,
   And sees a man in front of hit
Th'ow up his hands an' stagger—yes,—
     Tom Johnson 's quit."

LULLABY.

THE MAPLE strews the embers of its leaves
  O'er the laggard swallows nestled 'neath the eaves;
And the moody cricket falters in his cry—Baby-bye!—
And the lid of night is falling o'er the sky—Baby-bye!—
  The lid of night is falling o'er the sky!

The rose is lying pallid, and the cup
Of the frosted calla-lily folded up;
And the breezes through the garden sob and sigh—Baby-
    bye!—
O'er the sleeping blooms of summer where they lie—Baby-
    bye!—
  O er the sleeping blooms of summer where they lie!

Yet, Baby—O my Baby, for your sake
This heart of mine is ever wide awake,
And my love may never droop a drowsy eye—Baby-bye!—
Till your own are wet above me when I die—Baby-bye!—
  Till your own are wet above me when I die.

IN THE SOUTH.

THERE IS a princess in the South
  About whose beauty rumors hum
Like honey-bees about the mouth
    Of roses dewdrops falter from;
      And O her hair is like the fine
      Clear amber of a jostled wine
      In tropic revels; and her eyes
      Are blue as rifts of Paradise.

Such beauty as may none before
  Kneel daringly, to kiss the tips
Of fingers such as knights of yore
    Had died to lift against their lips:
      Such eyes as might the eyes of gold
      Of all the stars of night behold
      With glittering envy, and so glare
      In dazzling splendor of despair.

So, were I but a minstrel, deft
  At weaving, with the trembling strings
Of my glad harp, the warp and weft
    Of rondels such as rapture sings,—
      I 'd loop my lyre across my breast,
      Nor stay me till my knee found rest
      In midnight banks of bud and flower
      Beneath my lady's lattice-bower.

And there, drenched with the teary dews,
  I 'd woo her with such wondrous art
As well might stanch the songs that ooze
    Out of the mockbird's breaking heart;

So light, so tender, and so sweet
Should be the words I would repeat,
Her casement, on my gradual sight,
Would blossom as a lily might.

THE OLD HOME BY THE MILL.

THIS IS "The old Home by the Mill"—fer we still call it so,
Although the old mill, roof and sill, is all gone long ago.
The old home, though, and old folks, and the old spring, and a few
Old cat-tails, weeds and hartychokes, is left to welcome you!

Here, Marg'et, fetch the man a tin to drink out of! Our spring
Keeps kindo-sorto cavin' in, but do n't "taste" anything!
She's kindo agein', Marg'et is—"the old process," like me,
All ham-stringed up with rheumatiz, and on in seventy-three.

Jes' me and Marg'et lives alone here—like in long ago;
The childern all put off and gone, and married, do n't you know?
One's millin' way out West somewhere; two other miller-boys
In Minnyopolis they air; and one's in Illinoise.

The oldest gyrl—the first that went—married and died right here;
The next lives in Winn's Settlement—for purt' nigh thirty year!
And youngest one—was allus fer the old home here—but no!—
Her man turns in and he packs her 'way off to Idyho!

I do n't miss them like *Marg'et* does—'cause I got *her*, you see;

And when she pines for them—that 's 'cause *she's* only
    jes' got *me!*
I laugh, and joke her 'bout it all.—But talkin' sense, I 'll
    say,
When she was tuk so bad last Fall, I laughed the t'other
    way!

I haint so favor'ble impressed 'bout dyin'; but ef I
Found I was only second-best when *us two* come to die,
I 'd 'dopt the " new process " in full, ef *Marg'et* died, you
    see,—
I'd jes' crawl in my grave and pull the green grass over
    me!

A LEAVE-TAKING.

SHE will not smile;
　　She will not stir;
　I marvel while
　　I look on her.
　　　The lips are chilly
　　　　And will not speak;
　　　The ghost of a lily
　　　　In either cheek.

Her hair—ah me!
　　Her hair—her hair!
How helplessly
　　My hands go there!
　　　But my caresses
　　　　Meet not hers,
　　　O golden tresses
　　　　That thread my tears!

I kiss the eyes
　　On either lid,
Where her love lies
　　Forever hid.
　　　I cease my weeping
　　　　And smile and say:
　　　I will be sleeping
　　　　Thus, some day!

WAIT FOR THE MORNING.

WAIT for the morning:—It will come, indeed,
As surely as the night hath given need.
The yearning eyes, at last, will strain their sight
No more unanswered by the morning light;
No longer will they vainly strive, through tears,
To pierce the darkness of thy doubts and fears,
But, bathed in balmy dews and rays of dawn,
Will smile with rapture o'er the darkness drawn.

Wait for the morning, O thou smitten child,
Scorned, scourged and persecuted and reviled—
Athirst and famishing, none pitying thee,
Crowned with the twisted thorns of agony—
No faintest gleam of sunlight through the dense
Infinity of gloom to lead thee thence.—
Wait for the morning:—It will come, indeed,
As surely as the night hath given need.

WHEN JUNE IS HERE.

WHEN JUNE is here—what art have we to sing
The whiteness of the lilies midst the green
Of noon-tranced lawns? Or flash of roses seen
Like redbirds' wings? Or earliest ripening
Prince-Harvest apples, where the cloyed bees cling
Round winey juices oozing down between
The peckings of the robin, while we lean
In under-grasses, lost in marveling.
Or the cool term of morning, and the stir
Of odorous breaths from wood and meadow walks,
The bobwhite's liquid yodel, and the whir
Of sudden flight; and, where the milkmaid talks
Across the bars, on tilted barley-stalks
The dewdrops' glint in webs of gossamer.

The Gilded Roll

THE GILDED ROLL.

NOSING around in an old box—packed away, and lost to memory for years—an hour ago I found a musty package of gilt paper, or rather, a roll it was, with the green-tarnished gold of the old sheet for the outer wrapper. I picked it up mechanically to toss it into some obscure corner, when, carelessly lifting it by one end, a child's tin whistle dropped therefrom and fell tinkling on the attic floor. It lies before me on my writing table now—and so, too, does the roll entire, though now a roll no longer,—for my eager fingers have unrolled the gilded covering, and all its precious contents are spread out beneath my hungry eyes.

Here is a scroll of ink-written music. I don't read music, but I know the dash and swing of the pen that rained it on the page. Here is a letter, with the self-same impulse and abandon in every syllable; and its melody—however sweet the other—is far more sweet to me. And here are other letters like it—three—five—and seven, at least. Bob wrote them from the front, and Billy kept them for

me when I went to join him. Dear boy! Dear
boy!

Here are some cards of bristol-board. Ah!
when Bob came to these there were no blotches
then. What faces—what expressions! The
droll, ridiculous, good-for-nothing genius, with
his "sad mouth," as he called it, "upside
down," laughing always—at everything, at big
rallies, and mass-meetings and conventions,
county fairs, and floral halls, booths, water-
melon - wagons, dancing - tents, the swing,
Daguerrean-car, the "lung-barometer," and
the air-gun man. Oh! what a gifted, good-
for-nothing boy Bob was in those old days!
And here's a picture of a girlish face—a very
faded photograph—even fresh from "the gal-
lery," five and twenty years ago it was a faded
thing. But the living face—how bright and
clear that was!—for "Doc," Bob's awful
name for her, was a pretty girl, and brilliant,
clever, lovable every way. No wonder Bob
fancied her! And you could see some hint
of her jaunty loveliness in every fairy face he
drew, and you could find her happy ways and
dainty tastes unconsciously assumed in all he
did—the books he read—the poems he ad-
mired, and those he wrote; and, ringing clear
and pure and jubilant, the vibrant beauty of
her voice could clearly be defined and traced

through all his music. Now, there 's the
happy pair of them—Bob and Doc. Make
of them just whatever your good fancy may
dictate, but keep in mind the stern, relentless
ways of destiny.

You are not at the beginning of a novel,
only at the threshold of one of a hundred ex-
periences that lie buried in the past, and this
particular one most happily resurrected by
these odds and ends found in the gilded roll.

You see, dating away back, the contents of
this package, mainly, were hastily gathered together after a week's visit out at the
old Mills farm; the gilt paper, and the
whistle, and the pictures, they were Billy's;
the music pages, Bob's, or Doc's; the letters and some other manuscripts were mine.

The Mills girls were great friends of
Doc's, and often came to visit her in town;
and so Doc often visited the Mills's. This
is the way that Bob first got out there, and
won them all, and "shaped the thing" for
me, as he would put it; and lastly, we had
lugged in Billy,—such a handy boy, you
know, to hold the horses on pic-nic excursions, and to watch the carriage and the
luncheon, and all that.—"Yes, and," Bob
would say, "such a serviceable boy in getting
all the fishing tackle in proper order, and dig-

ging bait, and promenading in our wake up
and down the creek all day, with the minnow-
bucket hanging on his arm, do n't you know !"

But jolly as the days were, I think jollier
were the long evenings at the farm. After
the supper in the grove, where, when the
weather permitted, always stood the table,
ankle-deep in the cool green plush of the
sward ; and after the lounge upon the grass,
and the cigars, and the new fish stories, and
the general invoice of the old ones, it was de-
lectable to get back to the girls again, and in
the old " best room " hear once more the lilt
of the old songs and the stacattoed laughter
of the piano mingling with the alto and fal-
setto voices of the Mills girls, and the gallant
soprano of the dear girl Doc.

This is the scene I want you to look in
upon, as, in fancy, I do now—and here are
the materials for it all, husked from the gilded
roll :

Bob, the master, leans at the piano now,
and Doc is at the keys, her glad face
often thrown up sidewise toward his own.
His face is boyish—for there is yet but the
ghost of a mustache upon his lip. His eyes
are dark and clear, of over-size when looking
at you, but now their lids are drooped above
his violin, whose melody has, for the time, al-

most smoothed away the upward kinkings of
the corners of his mouth.   And wonderfully
quiet now is every one, and the chords of the
piano, too, are low and faltering; and so,
at last, the tune itself swoons into the uni-
versal hush, and—Bob is rasping, in its stead,
the ridiculous, but marvelously perfect imitation of the " priming " of a pump, while Billy's hands forget the " chiggers " on the bare
backs of his feet, as, with clapping palms, he
dances round the room in ungovernable
spasms of delight.   And then we all laugh;
and Billy, taking advantage of the general
tumult, pulls Bob's head down and whispers,
" Git 'em to stay up 'way late to-night!"
And Bob, perhaps remembering that we go
back home to-morrow, winks at the little fellow and whispers, " You let me manage 'em!
Stay up till broad daylight if we take a no-
tion—eh?"   And Billy dances off again in
newer glee, while the inspired musician is
plunking a banjo imitation on his enchanted
instrument, which is unceremoniously drowned
out by a circus-tune from Doc that is ab-
solutely inspiring to everyone but the bare-
footed brother, who drops back listlessly to his
old position on the floor and sullenly renews
operations on his " chigger " claims.

" Thought you was goin' to have pop-corn

to-night all so fast!" he says, doggedly, in the midst of a momentary lull that has fallen on a game of whist.   And then the oldest Mills girl, who thinks cards stupid anyhow, says: "That's so, Billy; and we're going to have it, too; and right away, for this game's just ending, and I sha n't submit to being bored with another.   I say 'pop-corn' with Billy! And after that," she continues, rising and addressing the party in general, " we must have another literary and artistic tournament, and that's been in contemplation and preparation long enough ; so you gentlemen can be pulling your wits together for the exercises, while us girls see to the refreshments."

"Have you done anything toward it!" queries Bob, when the girls are gone, with the alert Billy in their wake.

"Just an outline," I reply. "How with you?"

"Clean forgot it—that is, the preparation; but I 've got a little old second-hand idea, if you 'll all help me out with it, that 'll amuse us some, and tickle Billy I 'm certain."

So that 's agreed upon ; and while Bob produces his portfolio, drawing paper, pencils and so on, I turn to my note-book in a dazed way and begin counting my fingers in a depth of profound abstraction, from which I am

barely aroused by the reappearance of the
girls and Billy.

"Goody, goody, goody! Bob's goin' to
make pictures!" cries Billy, in additional trans-
port to that the cake pop-corn has produced.

"Now, you girls," says Bob, gently de-
taching the affectionate Billy from one leg and
moving a chair to the table, with a backward
glance of intelligence toward the boy,—"you
girls are to help us all you can, and we can
all work; but, as I'll have all the illustrations
to do, I want you to do as many of the verses
as you can—that'll be easy, you know,—because the work entire is just to consist of a
series of fool-epigrams, such as, for instance.—
Listen, Billy:

> Here lies a young man
> Who in childhood began
> To swear, and to smoke, and to drink,—
> In his twentieth year
> He quit swearing and beer,
> And yet is still smoking, I think."

And the rest of his instructions are deliv-
ered in lower tones, that the boy may not
hear; and then, all matters seemingly ar-
ranged, he turns to the boy with—"And now,
Billy, no lookin' over shoulders, you know,
or swinging on my chair-back while I'm at
work. When the pictures are all finished,

then you can take a squint at 'em, and not
before.   Is that all hunky, now?"

"Oh! who's a-goin' to look over your
shoulder—only *Doc*."   And as the radiant
Doc hastily quits that very post, and dives
for the offending brother, he scrambles under
the piano and laughs derisively.

And then a silence falls upon the group—a
gracious quiet, only intruded upon by the very
juicy and exuberant munching of an apple
from a remote fastness of the room, and the
occasional thumping of a bare heel against
the floor.

At last I close my note-book with a half
slam.

"That means," says Bob, laying down his
pencil, and addressing the girls, — "That
means he's concluded his poem, and that
he's not pleased with it in any manner, and
that he intends declining to read it, for that
self-acknowledged reason, and that he ex-
pects us to believe every affected word of his
entire speech—"

"Oh, do n't!" I exclaim.

"Then give us the wretched production, in
all its hideous deformity!"

And the girls all laugh so sympathetically,
and Bob joins them so gently, and yet with a
tone, I know, that can be changed so quickly

to my further discomfiture, that I arise at once
and read, without apology or excuse, this
primitive and very callow poem recovered
here to-day from the gilded roll:

A BACKWARD LOOK.

As I sat smoking, alone, yesterday,
   And lazily leaning back in my chair,
Enjoying myself in a general way—
Allowing my thoughts a holiday
   From weariness, toil and care,—
My fancies—doubtless, for ventilation—
   Left ajar the gates of my mind,—
And Memory, seeing the situation,
   Slipped out in street of "Auld Lang Syne."

Wandering ever with tireless feet
   Through scenes of silence, and jubilee
Of long-hushed voices; and faces sweet
Were thronging the shadowy side of the street
   As far as the eye could see;
Dreaming again, in anticipation,
   The same old dreams of our boyhood's days
That never come true, from the vague sensation
   Of walking asleep in the world's strange ways.

Away to the house where I was born!
   And there was the selfsame clock that ticked
From the close of dusk to the burst of morn,
When life-warm hands plucked the golden corn
   And helped when the apples were picked.
And the "chany-dog" on the mantel-shelf,
   With the gilded collar and yellow eyes,
Looked just as at first, when I hugged myself
   Sound asleep with the dear surprise.

And down to the swing in the locust tree,
　Where the grass was worn from the trampled ground,
And where "Eck" Skinner, "Old" Carr, and three
Or four such other boys used to be
　Doin' "sky-scrapers," or "whirlin' round:"
And again Bob climbed for the bluebird's nest,
　And again "had shows" in the buggy-shed
Of Guymon's barn, where still, unguessed,
　The old ghosts romp through the best days dead'

And again I gazed from the old school-room
　With a wistful look of a long June day,
When on my cheek was the hectic bloom
Caught of Mischief, as I presume—
　He had such a "partial" way,
It seemed, toward me.—And again I thought
　Of a probable likelihood to be
Kept in after school—for a girl was caught
　Catching a note from me.

And down through the woods to the swimming-hole—
　Where the big, white, hollow, old sycamore grows,—
And we never cared when the water was cold,
And always "ducked" the boy that told
　On the fellow that tied the clothes.—
When life went so like a dreamy rhyme,
　That it seems to me now that then
The world was having a jollier time
　Than it ever will have again.

The crude production is received, I am glad to note, with some expressions of favor from the company, though Bob, of course, must heartlessly dissipate my weak delight by saying, "Well, it's certainly bad enough; though," he goes on with an air of deepest critical

sagacity and fairness, "considered, as it
should be, justly, as the production of a jour-
poet, why, it might be worse—that is, a little
worse."

"Probably," I remember saying,—"Probably I might redeem myself by reading you
this little amateurish bit of verse, enclosed to
me in a letter by mistake, not very long ago."
I here fish an envelope from my pocket the
address of which all recognize as in Bob's
almost printed writing. He smiles vacantly
at it—then vividly colors.

"What date?" he stoically asks.

"The date," I suggestively answer, "of
your last letter to our dear Doc, at Boarding-
School, two days exactly in advance of her
coming home—this veritable visit now."

Both Bob and Doc rush at me—but too late.
The letter and contents have wholly vanished.
The youngest Miss Mills quiets us—urgently
distracting us, in fact, by calling our attention
to the immediate completion of our joint production ; "For now," she says, " with our new
reënforcement, we can, with becoming dili-
gence, soon have it ready for both printer and
engraver, and then we'll wake up the boy
(who has been fortunately slumbering for the
last quarter of an hour), and present to him, as
designed and intended, this matchless creation
of our united intellects." At the conclusion

of this speech we all go good-humoredly to work, and at the close of half an hour the tedious, but most ridiculous, task is announced completed.

As I arrange and place in proper form here on the table the separate cards—twenty-seven in number—I sigh to think that I am unable to transcribe for you the best part of the nonsensical work—the illustrations. All I can give is the written copy of—

BILLY'S ALPHABETICAL ANIMAL SHOW.

A was an elegant Ape
Who tied up his ears with red tape,
    And wore a long veil
    Half revealing his tail
Which was trimmed with jet bugles and crape.

B was a boastful old Bear
Who used to say,—" Hoomh! I declare
    I can eat—if you 'll get me
    The children, and let me—
Ten babies, teeth, toenails and hair!"

C was a Codfish who sighed
When snatched from the home of his pride,
    But could he, embrined,
    Guess this fragrance behind,
How glad he would be that he died!

D was a dandified Dog
Who said,—" Though it 's raining like fog
    I wear no umbrellah,
    Me boy, for a fellah
Might just as well travel incog!"

E WAS an elderly Eel
Who would say,—" Well, I really feel—
    As my grandchildren wriggle
    And shout 'I should giggle'—
A trifle run down at the heel!"

F WAS a Fowl who conceded
Some hens might hatch more eggs than *she* did,—
    But she'd children as plenty
    As eighteen or twenty,
And that was quite all that she needed.

G WAS a gluttonous Goat
Who, dining one day, *table-d'hote*,
    Ordered soup-bone, *au fait*,
    And fish, *papier-mache*,
And a *filet* of Spring overcoat.

H WAS a high-cultured Hound
Who could clear forty feet at a bound,
    And a coon once averred
    That his howl could be heard
For five miles and three-quarters around.

I WAS an Ibex ambitious
To dive over chasms auspicious;
    He would leap down a peak
    And not light for a week,
And swear that the jump was delicious.

J WAS a Jackass who said
He had such a bad cold in his head,
    If it was n't for leaving
    The rest of us grieving,
He 'd really rather be dead.

K was a profligate Kite
Who would haunt the saloons every night;
   And often he ust
   To reel back to his roost
Too full to set up on it right.

L was a wary old Lynx
Who would say,—" Do you know wot I thinks?—
   I thinks ef you happen
   To ketch me a-nappin'
I 'm ready to set up the drinks!"

M was a merry old Mole,
Who would snooze all the day in his hole,
   Then—all night, a-rootin'
   Around and galootin'—
He 'd sing "Johnny, Fill up the Bowl!"

N was a caustical Nautilus
Who sneered, "I suppose, when they 've *caught*
   all us,
   Like oysters they 'll serve us,
   And can us, preserve us,
And barrel, and pickle, and bottle us!"

O was an autocrat Owl—
Such a wise—such a wonderful fowl!
   Why, for all the night through
   He would hoot and hoo-hoo,
And hoot and hoo-hooter and howl!

P was a Pelican pet,
Who gobbled up all he could get;
   He could eat on until
   He was full to the bill,
And there he had lodgings to let!

Q WAS a querulous Quail,
Who said: "It will little avail
The efforts of those
Of my foes who propose
To attempt to put salt on my tail!"

R WAS a ring-tailed Raccoon,
With eyes of the tinge of the moon,
And his nose a blue-black,
And the fur on his back
A sad sort of sallow maroon.

S IS a Sculpin—you'll wish
Very much to have one on your dish,
    Since all his bones grow
    On the outside, and so
He's a very desirable fish.

T WAS a Turtle, of wealth,
Who went round with particular stealth,—
    "Why," said he, "I'm afraid
    Of being waylaid
When I even walk out for my health!"

U WAS a Unicorn curious,
With one horn, of a growth so *luxurious*,
    He could level and stab it—
    If you did n't grab it—
Clean through you, he was so blamed furious!

V WAS was a vagabond Vulture
Who said: "I do n't want to insult yer,
    But when you intrude
    Where in lone solitude
I'm a-preyin', you're no man o' culture!"

W was a wild *Wood*chuck,
And you can just bet that he *could* "chuck "—
   He 'd eat raw potatoes,
   Green corn, and tomatoes,
And tree roots, and call it all "*good* chuck!"

X was a kind of X-cuse
Of a some-sort-o'-thing that got loose
   Before we could name it,
   And cage it, and tame it,
And bring it in general use.

Y is the Yellowbird,—bright
As a petrified lump of star-light,
   Or a handful of lightning-
   Bugs, squeezed in the tight'ning
Pink fist of a boy, at night.

Z is the Zebra, of course!—
A kind of a clown-of-a-horse,—
   Each other despising,
   Yet neither devising
A way to obtain a divorce!

& here is the famous—what-is-it?
Walk up, Master Billy, and quiz it:
   You 've seen the *rest* of 'em—
   Ain't this the *best* of 'em,
Right at the end of your visit?

At last Billy is sent off to bed. It is the prudent mandate of the old folks : But so lothfully the poor child goes, Bob's heart goes,
too.—Yes, Bob himself, to keep the little fellow company awhile, and, up there under the
old rafters, in the pleasant gloom, lull him to

famous dreams with fairy tales. And it is
during this brief absence that the youngest
Mills girl gives us a surprise. She will read a
poem, she says, written by a very dear friend
of hers who, fortunately for us, is not present
to prevent her. We guard door and window
as she reads. Doc says she will not listen;
but she does listen, and cries, too—out of pure
vexation, she asserts. The rest of us, however, cry just because of the apparent honesty
of the poem of—

BEAUTIFUL HANDS.

O your hands—they are strangely fair!
Fair—for the jewels that sparkle there,—
Fair—for the witchery of the spell
That ivory keys alone can tell;
But when their delicate touches rest
Here in my own do I love them best,
As I clasp with eager acquisitive spans
My glorious treasure of beautiful hands!

Marvelous—wonderful—beautiful hands!
They can coax roses to bloom in the strands
Of your brown tresses; and ribbons will twine,
Under mysterious touches of thine,
Into such knots as entangle the soul,
And fetter the heart under such a control
As only the strength of my love understands—
My passionate love for your beautiful hands.

As I remember the first fair touch
Of those beautiful hands that I love so much,
I seem to thrill as I then was thrilled,
Kissing the glove that I found unfilled—

When I met your gaze, and the queenly bow,
As you said to me, laughingly, "Keep it now!"
And dazed and alone in a dream I stand
Kissing this ghost of your beautiful hand.

When first I loved, in the long ago,
And held your hand as I told you so—
Pressed and carressed it and gave it a kiss,
And said "I could die for a hand like this!"
Little I dreamed love's fulness yet
Had to ripen when eyes were wet,
And prayers were vain in their wild demands
For one warm touch of your beautiful hands.

Beautiful Hands! O Beautiful Hands!
Could you reach out of the alien lands
Where you are lingering, and give me, to-night,
Only a touch—were it ever so light—
My heart were soothed, and my weary brain
Would lull itself into rest again;
For there is no solace the world commands
Like the caress of your beautiful hands.

*   *   *   *   *.   *   *

Violently winking at the mist that blurs my sight, I regretfully awaken to the here and now. And is it possible, I sorrowfully muse, that all this glory can have fled away?—that more than twenty long, long years are spread between me and that happy night? And is it possible that all the dear old faces—O, quit it! quit it! Gather the old scraps up and wad 'em back into oblivion, where they belong!

Yes, but be calm—be calm! Think of

cheerful things. You are not all alone. *Bil-ly*'s living yet.

I know—and six feet high—and sag-shouldered—and owns a tin and stove-store, and can't hear thunder! *Billy!*

And the youngest Mills girl—she's alive, too.

S'pose I don't know that? I married her! And Doc.—

Bob married her. Been in California for more than fifteen years—on some blasted cattle-ranch, or something,- and he's worth a half a million! And am I less prosperous with this gilded roll?

www.ingramcontent.com/pod-product-compliance
Lightning Source LLC
Chambersburg PA
CBHW030537040726
47497CB00008B/2490